NO EXIT
Julie Burchill

Mandarin

A Mandarin Paperback
NO EXIT

First published in Great Britain 1993
by Sinclair-Stevenson
This edition published 1993
by Mandarin Paperbacks
an imprint of Reed Consumer Books Ltd
Michelin House, 81 Fulham Road, London SW3 6RB
and Auckland, Melbourne, Singapore and Toronto

Reprinted 1993

A CIP catalogue record for this title
is available from the British Library
ISBN 0 7493 1326 9

Printed and bound in Great Britain by
BPCC Paperbacks Ltd

Member of BPCC Ltd

For Antoine
and Jane

1

You could take the boy out of the Eighties – but you couldn't take the Eighties out of the boy, Gary First reflected smugly as he looked into his Macintosh IIci4/80 as though it was a mirror. Which in a way it was – 'Mirror is non-U for Macintosh,' Gary I quipped, causing Gary II much mirth. The Mac threw back exactly the image he wanted to see; it told him he was young, sussed and earning enough at the age of twenty-five to render a five thousand pound computer merely another affordable little luxury.

If it had been a looking-glass proper, it would have also told Gary First something else he was already far too well aware of; that he was gorgeous. Not handsome, or pretty, or attractive – but gorgeous, like Marilyn Monroe.

His dark glossy hair rose in a full smooth quiff, like an American retro ad dream, from a bulging baby's brow. His glossy black brows and lashes were of the quality and quantity that supermodels spent hours in salons achieving by means of dye and tattoo. His nose was even shorter than his temper – and a good deal straighter than his nature, in the days when straight meant honest rather than heterosexual. His eyes were dark blue and his mouth pouting pink. He had a peculiar skin of an ivory tint so creamy that it sometimes looked – especially in black and white photographs – almost dark.

Since he was twelve years old, older men had been aiming cameras at him in the street. Some of them probably contained film and some definitely didn't. Since he had grown so tall – six one at the age of twenty, – he could usually scare them off with a look. But growing up he had been all too aware, without ever really putting it into words, of the sort of garbage women have to take from eye-balling men every day of the week, and it had made him to some extent sensitive to women's feelings of vulnerability to strangers without ever making him sensitive to women's vulnerability to those they loved. He broke girls' hearts regularly – but he would never have dreamed of whistling at one. If you thought about it too long, perhaps it was a weird morality. But it worked for him.

He didn't have too many complaints, anyway. 'God, you look like Clive – whatisname? On TV!' a Norwegian girl called Tone had once told him in bed. He had grinned knowingly, raising a silky eyebrow – but inside his self-possessed body his heart was doing a routine worthy of early Gene Krupa. He didn't watch much television, and the only Clive he could think of was the bald berk with the bad voice. He put Tone's gaff down to her foreignness. But he was much relieved, later that month, when she dragged him over to an old film poster in Athena and he saw a familiar boy beauty called Clive Owen smiling conspiratorially down at him.

He squinted at the screen, while beside him a

still-life by Bartle Bogle Hegarty composed itself;
a Mexican beer with a twist of lime stuck in its
throat and a slice of gourmet pizza stared thoughtfully at a copy of *Arena*, which was open at a quiz
which would tell them if they were New Men or
not. Fearing that it would merely confirm them to
be a bottle of beer and a lump of designer dough,
they pursued the matter no further.

Gary knew no such fear; it was boredom, not
self-doubt, which had left the quiz uncompleted.
He preferred surveys, anyway; it was his habit,
upon coming across magazine readership surveys,
to turn straight to the salary boxes, tick OVER
£50,000, fill in his name, age and address and
send it off. One such communiqué to the *New
Statesman and Society* had received a reply which
belied the rag's promise of discretion and ano-
nymity: the very same copy of the survey with DIE
RICH SCUM scrawled across it in envious green
Dayglo. It was the first time anyone had called
him rich scum – him, the boy from the cul-de-sac!
– and it felt damn good.

The computer screen showed him a short list,
which was par for the course. 'Lists are the haiku
of the ambitious,' his ex-girlfriend Miranda had

4

once said – and it had stuck in his mind, which was more than Miranda herself had. She was a nice Holland Park girl – a bit too nice, which was bad news when the doors were double-locked, the Artemide spotlights were shining on the futon and there was the best part of a week's wages worth of La Perla hanging in the wardrobe. But she had been a not unpleasant part of his education; they had trolled around Tuscany, read Ian McEwan novels (quite raunchy in parts) and wasted good-sized chunks of their one and only lives choosing between five sorts of lettuce, for fuck's sake, on the clean streets of Notting Hill. And of course they'd had fairly unmemorable sex, as you did with a girl who could get orgasmic over greens. ('Do you really feel compelled to use that word?' 'What's wrong with it?' 'I feel it has a history. A pungency that isn't altogether pleasant.' 'Are you trying to tell me I've got sweaty nuts?' '*Please*, Gary.' Yes, she was a right little stand-up, old Miranda, and she didn't appreciate *that* witty little riposte *at all*. He wouldn't have minded if 'that word' had been 'twat' or 'shag', but he'd only *said* 'nooky'.) Until he met Nikki. Thank God for Essex girls.

Fate and a perfect figure had led Nikki from Dagenham to Stringfellows, where Gary watched her gyrate in form-fitting garb which he thought of as Spandex Simplex when he should have been collecting material for a high-handed and somewhat unpleasant newspaper feature called, 'Killer Bimbos At Ease'.

'If you had a handbag, you'd dance around it,' he told Nikki as he reached, unasked, across the bar and paid the barman for the Aqua Libre and Stoly she'd just palmed.

'No I wouldn't,' she said in a high, light, cool Cockney voice. 'I'd hit you round the head with it.'

Gary gaped at her as she slid off her barstool and ambulated primly towards a table where a brace of Basildonian babes sat bantering. He was a boy of the proletarian blood royal himself, and had only abandoned his sisters in the struggle because they seemed to turn so stolid, passive and stupid the minute they hit – or rather, got mugged by – puberty. To find a pretty prole who wasn't lumpen – and had a *figure* to boot, a real Fifties extravaganza, in an age when girls as a rule had rather morbid-sounding *bodies* – was a wet dream come true. He slipped off his stool, straightened his Georgina von Etzdorf tie and high-tailed it after her.

At the table, Nikki was sipping her mould-breaking cocktail and watching the dancers abstractedly while her friends talked intensely. They were at that stage of extreme drunkenness which is unique to pretty and semi-smart working-class girls and is marked by monologues, quotes from Tina Turner songs, physical contact verging on the Sapphic and analysis of the male sex which is three parts banal to one part genius.

'D'you know, Stacey, what the name of the game is?' the gorgeous Anglo-Caribbean girl with skin like Kahlúa and cream and the long poker-straight black ponytail pulled back from a brow of MENSA dimensions was asking the gorgeous Anglo-Italian girl with skin like Bailey's Irish Cream and long shimmering waves of black hair falling over her bare shoulders above the scarlet boob tube.

'No, Talitha – tell me!' gasped Stacey, eyes wide with wonder at her friend's wisdom. As he watched them, Gary realised with the reptilian eye of the lecher and the observant eye of the journal-ist that Stacey was in love with Talitha, and would

7

never tell her, and would marry a self-adoring Cypriot with a car showroom in Great Portland Street, and would hate herself, and would have an affair with a lifeguard in Lanzarote, and would lose custody of her two children (Emma, 7, and Alexander, 3) and would take to drink of an evening on the terrace of her divorcée's villa on the Costas, and would run to fat, and would love Talitha, as she was in the here and now, forever – and she would never tell her. Stacey's life, not waving but drowning, passed before Gary's eyes in the space of sixty seconds.

He had the maddest impulse to step forward and tell the girls they were celestial twins, and should not fight their love. But they would have merely written him off as a masher in the mood for a little diversionary muff-diving – which was probably partially true, as it was of ninety-five per cent of men at least seventy per cent of the time, if you wanted to be all cold and analytical about it. So he held his piece, in silence.

'The name of the game – is – *survival*,' pronounced the immaculate Talitha slowly, and her dark profound head and Stacey's moved a millimetre closer to happiness.

Gary wrenched his eyes back to the bolshy blonde babe who had led him to this little corner of Stringfellows which would be forever Lesbos. She had transparently chosen her companions for their colouring, which made her stand out like living mercury against black velvet. Usually pretty girls chose plain friends to make them look even prettier, but at this level of social activity such an option was no longer possible. So Nikki had settled for a pair of perfect brunettes.

Some are born blonde, some achieve blondeness and some have blondeness thrust upon them by their modelling agencies, thought Gary in Style Page-speak; it would later transpire that Nikki was a real blonde, even fairer than her assumed golden, but had moved down a notch from her natural platinum, 'So I don't look too dumb'. Personally, Gary thought this was shutting the door after the whore had bolted. But he kept it to himself.

Sighing, still watching the dancers, Nikki crossed and uncrossed her legs which was rather like watching a sexed-up Tower Bridge go through its smooth moves. She had a level of thoroughbred beauty which rarely chooses to garb itself in skintight Spandex and slingbacks, her exaggeratedly long limbs and sharp-chinned, narrow face combining almost freakishly with her sumptuous torso. The effect was shattering.

He walked over to the table and stood in front of Nikki; Stacey and Talitha were off in orbit, no trouble. She looked up at him, pouting warily – or was it wearily? – and he indicated the empty fourth chair.

'Can I sit down?' he mouthed above a blaring *Sexual Healing*; clearly the club was in under-stated, modest mode tonight.

'I don't know. Can you? I would have thought your trousers were too tight.' Nikki threw up her sharp little chin and screeched with auto-amusement.

Gary showed his teeth manfully, trying for a self-deprecating grin. He calculated he had man-aged it but then a young woman passing close by glanced at him and gave a muffled scream. Must try harder. He sat across the chair, legs either side, chin resting on his arms resting along the back, and stared at her sincerely. 'I won't insult you by telling you how beautiful you are.'

'Thanks.' She pulled a cigarette from a soft,

posh packet on the table and put it between her lips. She glared at Gary. He grinned back. After thirty seconds she removed the cigarette and laughed.

'Aren't you going to light me?'

'I wouldn't insult you.'

'Jeez – you won't tell me I'm beautiful, you won't light my fag; if you're coming on like this so as not to insult me, how the fuck do you behave when you *want* to insult someone?'

They glared at each other for a moment, still locked in pre-coital combat, before relaxing and laughing together for the first time. It was a good laugh, long and loud. Afterwards Gary lit Nikki's cigarette, and one for himself.

'The cigarette afterwards is always the best thing about a good giggle, innit?' sparkled Nikki, leaning forward to receive the Zippo's benediction. 'So what d'you do, when you're not trying to pick up smart-ass blondes in nightclubs?' She sounded genuinely interested.

'I'm a journalist.' It still gave him a sharp, black-and-white movie thrill of urban-jungle pride, even after seven years.

'Yeah?' Nikki had had one too many bad

11

experiences with *Daily Star* hacks who had failed to make their excuses and leave, he could tell. 'Who for?'

'*The Mail on Sunday.*'

'You're not!' She looked amused. 'Prove it!'

He took out his press card from its customary place next to his heart and handed it to her.

'Ga-ry … First,' she read slowly, squinting in the darkness. A false eyelash fell on to his hand and he yelped. She looked down, laughed and swiped it back, giving him his card. 'Is that your real name?'

'Course. Why not?'

'It's a good name. A bit different. I thought it might be a stage name.'

'But I'm not an actor.'

'You're a journalist, aren't you? We're both in showbiz.'

Nikki was a struggling model – though her likelihood of struggling *too* hard decreased in exact ratio to the rising importance of the photographer. A little too off-centre for mainstream Anglo-American taste nourished on the melting

Madonna-ish darkness of Yasmin Le Bon and Christy Turlington and the teeth-and-smiles wholesome blondeness of Claudia Schiffer and Christie Brinkley, she was forever jetting off to Munich or Tokyo to do something Not Quite Nice, returning with ever bigger bottles of duty-free Eau Sauvage Extreme and ever briefer pieces of underwear.

She was a great girl – sexy, sassy and street-smart. All the things you'd look for in a bottle of scent. But he'd been with her for six months, and he wasn't sure if he could restrict himself indefinitely to a woman whose lips, however sweet and skilful, moved when she read *Hello!* Still, she *was* a great girl. Miranda, too. Chalk and cheese, coke and Camembert – but great girls. In fact, Gary had only one thing against them; they were women. And as was their wont, after a certain sequence of shagging and dinner parties, they wanted something called a 'relationship'. As the word implied, this made them not so much your bird as one of your relations. In other words, it made them a right royal pain in the BTM who gobbled up time and energy like there was no tomorrow.

Thus the bottom line – on Gary's beautiful computer, beneath

SUBLET
CANCEL PAPERS
PASSPORT READY
ARMANI SUIT – GET!

which was

LOSE NIKKI

He reached for the phone and punched out Nikki's Fulham number, thanking J. Christos Esq that Nikki was in Fulham, and not in Holborn with him; then it would be *her* doing the punching out. She was a boxer's daughter, a precious only child, and had been trained from infancy to protect her honour by her old man, a well-meaning old fascist from Haggerston.

'Hello?' Softly, softly; Nikki was in phone-sex mode. It might be Bob Carlos Clarke on the line.

'Nikki? Gary. How are ya, gel?' (The 'g' was hard, like life.)

'As well as I was when you last asked me, darling. Which was three weeks ago.' The sex exited.

'Yeah, I know.' Gary sighed soulfully. 'Sorry

14

about that. Work. A lot of changes going down.'

'For THREE WEEKS!' Nikki's voice moved an octave north and several postal codes east simultaneously.

'Yeah, right. I said I'm sorry. I've been a naughty boy.' Gary fidgeted irritably with his keyboard, and without meaning to typed the word SLAG next to Nikki's name. LOSE NIKKI SLAG. He blinked at it, surprised, and wiped the word quickly. The New Man quiz stared at him, reeking of monochromatic moral revulsion. 'But listen to this – I've cracked it. I got that job I wanted, remember? That radio job? Czechoslovakia, for the World Service! Two years! And after that it could be Moscow, Washington – you name it.' He paused to let her congratulate him; give and take, and respecting the other person's right to speak was a crucial element in men/women relationships, he knew.

There was a silence, almost unbearably sleek in its chic minimalism. Gary always felt that the silences he heard on his own beautiful Bakelite were somehow technically superior to the silences heard on bog-standard BT phones; designer silence, if you will. He broke it reluctantly.

'Nikki?'

She sounded sulky, like she'd lost a pound and gained a stone. 'Congratulations.'

'What's wrong?'

'Nothing.'

'J. Christos, gel! I thought you'd be pleased for me!'

That was it. Nikki came off the ropes, swinging. Haggerston would have been proud of her. 'I might be a bit more pleased, you thoughtless bastard, if *you* didn't sound so bloody pleased at the thought of putting thousands of miles between us!'

There was another blissful beat of designer silence, during which a look of real distaste crossed Gary First's face. As though he had found a pube in his polenta.

Then a sly smile saw it off smartish, and his voice was so sweet it should have given Nikki a sugar rush. 'Six hundred and fifty miles, actually.'

In Fulham, a red Trimfone shattered with the impact of its return to its final resting place, and three flatmates with names ending in i's and eyes ending in tears had their girls' night in ruined by repeated recitations of the exact circumstances of

The End of Nikki's Thing With Gary. Just before dawn, they finally slept.

In home sweet Holborn, Gary smiled at his phone for a moment before replacing the black Bakelite beauty with Japanese delicacy, shaking his head more in sorrow than in anger.

'Some people – self, self, *self*!'

He laughed – half at himself, half at Nikki, though for very different reasons – took a mouthful of pizza, a swig of Sol, and wiped the last line from the haiku.

2

Gary First worked for *The Mail on Sunday,* the most strikingly success-ful newspaper in England and therefore the world. It was partly this fact which had helped him decide to branch out into broadcasting; after the *MOS,* other papers were just pâté. The broadsheets who would have killed for its readership profile and ad-vertising revenue were deadly dull and phoney; the tabloids who would have committed daylight robbery – and often did – for its nous and cred were moronic and moribund. Steering a middle course between hard news and high style, it was the singular triumph of the Nineties newspaper medium.

But after five years there, Gary First needed a change of scene and broadcasting, while paying peanuts, still had the lure of Graham Greene, the Third Man, Mel Gibson and above all the getting of wisdom. Gary knew he could coast forever on his good looks and handsome salary, but he feared becoming settled before he was even formed. He was a callow youth in all but one thing; he was well aware of how callow he was. So he was giving up *that* salary and *that* lifestyle, and starting all over again.

'Excellent,' said his editor when Gary told him this. 'Every young man should travel. Like acne and a love of bad translations of Nietzsche, abroad is a phase we must pass through with as much grace and haste as we can muster. I happen to have, at home, some fascinating books on that part of the world – I shall bring them in tomorrow.'

There were only two bad things about the boss, Gary reflected as he sat at his desk throughout yet another lunchtime – his vast library and his impeccably generous nature when it came to guiding the careers of his cubs. Proof of both, in the shape of two huge dusty tomes, sat in front of him. But the worst was past.

The huge office was empty – apart from one rakish hack, a Byronic boy in a business suit, suitably named Max. He was aiming straight for Gary, a spring in his step and a gleam in his eye, and he was carrying a box.

'Yo, Boy Wonder.' He perched on Gary's desk, nodding at the books. 'How's it hanging?'

Gary slumped back and lit a Marlboro with a shaky hand.

'Ku Klux Klan,' tutted Max, automatically, being of the Conspiracy Theory Generation.

Gary laughed. 'Research? I can handle it. You should have seen it before the weekend.' He leaned across the desk, looking smug. 'I've been at it for twenty-four hours straight – Stewart's been great. Ask me anything you want to know about Czechoslovakia and the Czechs. Or the Slovaks.'

Max plucked the cigarette from Gary's lips, inhaled and considered. 'How do you say "Sit on my face"?' he finally asked.

21

'International language, innit?'

Max smirked obscenely, but gestured in a decent way towards the books. 'So you're down to these, that right?'

Gary grinned and nodded, so smugly that his own mother would have itched to slap him silly.

'Good.' Max delved into the box and brought forth half a dozen bulky books, which he piled with the glee of a child into a high-rise horror on to the desk. 'Stewart thought you might like to give these babies a quick dekko.' Again his handsome face was split by a smile like a bacon-slicer. 'Maybe you'll find "Sit on my face" in one of them, eh?'

With a piercing cry of anguish, Gary First fell face-first into his background reading.

After dark, he sat in the Groucho reading *The Modern Review* and wishing Marco would get a move on.

Marco was the best he could do when it came to best friends, though the boy himself would have stuck two fingers down his throat and retched righteously had the subject been broached. He was a young man of uncertain origins and dubious Futures who, like Gary, had dedicated a good part of his life to keeping the spirit of the Eighties alive. No caring, sharing, phoney baloney for Marco; no biologically degradable lifestyle choices for *him*. Marco always swore that the only biologically degradable items *he* had time for were *women*.

He could be – what you mean, white boy, *could be!* – crude, and to the naked car offensive; Paki, Chinky, pussy, Wop (he was a Wop himself, and proud of it; therefore, he reasoned, pussy and Paki should be proud of being what *they* were). But, as with a chosen few of his kind, his surface brashness protected a basic decency (Marco was the only man Gary knew who habitually gave beggars fifty pound notes when stark-staring sober) which was often totally lacking in the professionally Nice.

Here he was now, his honest, broad, big-boned Italian face seeming surprised to find itself being flown above the body of a Big Bang Boy (sounds like a pop group, Gary thought) decked out in all its vulgar, vital glory; red braces embellished with dollar signs, striped shirt, Armani suit. Marco wore enough hair gel to cause a major oil slick

23

should he go swimming in the sea, and enough designer stubble to provoke a scolding from the EEC should he be silly enough to try to scorch it off. But he had heart, and he was home – home's not where we come from but where we choose to go – and Gary smiled with sheer relish as Marco sunk into a sofa, complaining.

'They made me leave my phone in reception – can you credit the barbarism of these people? Where do they get off, that's what I'd like to know. Where's their morals? "You wouldn't ask a bloke with a dodgy ticker to leave his pacemaker at the door, would you?" I said to the dopey slag behind the desk. "No, sir." "Well, that's what this little darling is!" I told her. "It's my life-support machine." ' Marco stopped, grinned at Gary and looked around with studied ennui. 'Late, am I?'

'Yeah. Unfashionably so. *Very* Eighties.'

'Can I help it if I'm in demand from dawn till dusk?' Marco was still casing the joint, sizing up lone women the way a burglar looks at putative possessions. 'Oh no, look at the legs on *that*! Of course, legs are a girl's best friend – but even best friends have to part sometime.' He signalled a waitress in vain, pretended he'd been waving at the godlike Liam, the club's kingpin, instead and turned back to Gary. 'So what's the action like in Czechoslovakia, then? Come on, I seen that film – the dirty one with the bird in the top hat and suspenders. Unbearable something – didn't look too unbearable to me!' He finally waylaid a waitress. 'Get us a Sapporo, sweetheart. But be sure to hold it at arm's length – I want it *cold.*' He cackled complacently as the tough teenager gave him a withering look and walked off. 'Gets 'em every time!'

Gary shook his head lovingly, as Marco wanted him to, and downed an olive. '*The Unbearable Lightness Of Being.* Lena Olin. She's a Swede, though.'

'That's right?' Marco was still rubber-necking. 'What about that lezzie tennis player, then? Stap me! Wouldn't like to meet *that* up a dark strasse with a stiletto in its shoe!'

'That was Rosa Klebb. Russian.' Gary drank deep from his beer as Marco received his. Then he leaned closer to his friend. 'Listen, the women there can be card-carrying dykes with ideological armpits to a man, for all I care. I'm not going there to get my end away; I'm going there to give this job one hundred and one per cent of my time, talent and testosterone.' He drank again. 'I just cut Nikki loose last week. She wasn't best pleased.'

Marco rolled his eyes to the heavens, or at least the Soho Rooms. 'Women!'

'It's just so much *hassle*.' Gary was a little drunk and maudlin by now, and was therefore using Seventies slang popular at a time when he had been busy playing with his Action Man. 'Even for a so-so thing. You know, Marco – I'm really starting to believe that men *can't* have it all – the hot career *and* the fine romance. We were conned. *Something's* got to give.'

'Yeah – *they* give, *you* take. And that's the way it should be. You're too sensitive, mate – treat 'em mean and keep 'em keen. That New Man crap was last year.' His roving eye hit paydirt. 'Oi, look at the blonde tuna at the bar – designer dyke if ever I saw it! Want to witness an instant conversion?'

Laughter lanced the censoriousness that was on the tip of his tongue. 'Marco! You're incorrigible! Don't you ever give it a rest?'

'Who, me?' Marco slumped back, wide-eyed,

pointing at himself. 'Rest? Rest, when there are songs to be sung, blow to be snorted and slappers to be saveloyed?' Without warning, his voice changed completely. 'Rest, when you're a nice public schoolboy from Sussex, with a Double First you're going to have to spend the rest of your life living down?' Marco clapped him on the shoulder, sportif, and looked at him, deadly serious. 'Gaz, old mate, you don't know how lucky you are. Born with nothing – born to travel light.' He gripped Gary's chin, and stared him urgently in the eye. 'Let's keep it that way, eh?'

Three nightclubs and two magnums later, Gary found himself alone on Waterloo Bridge. Crossing from the South Bank, the cliché-proof beauty of the view stopped him dead in his stumbling drunk tracks, and he leaned on the rail and looked towards the Savoy.

When men of a certain age talk about London, he thought, there's this certain tone of voice they have – I can't explain it properly, but I only hear it one place else. It's the voice men usually reserve for telling tales about their ex-wives: 'The bitch took my youth, drained my juice, bled me dry and dumped me!'

London never lives up to her promises. And worse, she makes you bloody aware that you never live up to *yours*. When you look at a map of the world, it should be so *easy* to conquer a little bitty city like this one. Easy just to knock it on the head, throw it over your shoulder and drag it home for déjeuner at your bijou cave in Holborn. But it's not.

I was one of the lost tribe of London; the kids from the sticks who sleep with a map of the Underground over their bed. Notting Hill Gate, Holland Park, White City – the stations of the cross! I got through the agonising limbo (is that an oxymoron?) of my teenage years by believing that London would belong to me one day. But she doesn't.

Because London – she's a whore. Like her sister-in-law Lady Luck – always looking over your shoulder for a higher bidder, even as you take her in your arms for the betrothal kiss. Always on heat for the highest roller. So I never really got to her. Just trod water – albeit in Bass Weejuns. And I've already used up half my twenties. The loose change of my life is running low. Must write that down. Good line.

Like a man attempting to molest himself on a public highway, Gary's completely uncoordinated hands dove drunkenly inside his jacket, fumbling for something to write on and with. Am I drunk? he asked himself, just before finding his Filofax. Got it. What was it, now?

Inspiration had flown. Instead Gary gaped dumbly at the little book which had symbolised his success. Once he had worshipped it. 'You know on *Desert Island Discs*? What book would you take besides the Bible and Shakespeare? It should be besides the Bible, Shakespeare and your Filofax.' But now, at his stage of crapulous cretinism, the benign and useful little book looked like *The Protocols of the Elders of Zion, Mein Kampf* and the latest Jeffrey Archer all rolled into one. That is, it looked *bad*. As in *not good*.

Look at this, Gary flourished rhetorically and silently, holding the despised item in both hands. *Look at this*! The stinking symbol of a decade when people were 'contacts'. Friendships were 'lunch'. And love was a 'relationship'. Well, not for me! He shook his head, still staring at the little book. God, I'll be glad to leave this rotten town. Before it bleeds me dry. He threw the Filofax up into the air; the lights of the Embankment twinkled heartbreakingly behind it.

'Good riddance, London! *Bon chance*, Eighties!' The Filofax hit the water just before Gary hit the ground.

'Allright! I'll tell you! Anything you want!'

Something had happened. Sometime overnight, a gang of balaclavad SAS men had entered Gary First's Holborn flat and with amazing stealth had removed him in an unmarked van to a Government research centre in darkest Berkshire where even this minute scientists who derived a good deal of job satisfaction were finessing even more ruthless and repulsive torments to break down the enemy and make him sing like Pavarotti.

As luck would have it, Gary First had been chosen in some secret state ballot to stand in for the genuine enemy, who might be round to the NCCL sharpish straight after checking out. And through an artful combination of white noise, a triple enema and multiple blows to the head, Gary

First was now ready to tell the nice men everything. Including details of *both* his run-ins with impotence, and the time he'd been sat by the toilets at the Caprice.

He opened his eyes slowly, fearful of what stray splatters of himself he might see on the walls. But instead he found himself staring at his *Terminator 2* poster – Arnie with Uzi on high-handled hog. Opening out, the vista showed off-white walls and black ash bedroom furniture, and a window framing an autumn view of Coram Fields.

Which meant he was at home. The bastards hadn't even bothered to take him to some sort of final resting place!

He tried to sit up, and failed. Flat on his back, he began to realise that what he was suffering was simply the hugest hangover he had ever had. The relief that he was not in Berkshire was fast followed by another bolt of panic, albeit of a recognisable kind; the Missing Jigsaw Piece, the morning-after feeling known to all those who drink seriously.

He could remember the Groucho. He could remember the champagne. But there was something just out of the frame. He had committed some appalling gaffe. But what was it? Had he been rude to Stewart? Had he, perish the thought, tried it on with Marco in the back of a taxi between clubs? Impossible, he wouldn't be in one piece. Had he, please God no, got off with some girl and notched up yet another bout of brewer's droop?

Suddenly it hit him. He sat bolt upright in his bed.

'MY FAX! MY BEAUTIFUL FAX!'

In despair, he clapped a hand flat out against his forehead with some force. The resulting pain made him feel that the nice men in the white coats in darkest Berkshire might actually be a preferable option.

3

The most beautiful girl in Bohemia got home before dusk that late afternoon to the apartment in Pardubice where her parents lived with her two younger sisters all the time (probably unto infinity, she told herself grimly as she struggled into the cage lift with her small suitcase and three shopping bags) and where she lived from Friday evening till Monday morning. Pardubice was only sixty miles away from Prague. But those sixty miles might have been thirty years. Nothing had changed.

She had worked through her lunch hour and shopped on her way to the station to surprise her parents with a smorgasbord supper when they got back from the plant. They would be there until seven; her sisters would arrive back here with them around seven-thirty after being picked up from the after-school centre they attended. They would all be pleased to see the food – but even more pleased to see *her*; an unusual set of priorities in the new Czechoslovakia, she smirked to herself.

During the week she lived officially in a Prague hostel for young professional women. The problem was that more and more young professional women in Prague these days were prostitutes, and the hostel was the one condition her reasonable and rather open-minded parents had insisted on when she moved to the city. They would have been very surprised – more surprised even than by their incipient supper! – to discover that their first-born spent at least three nights a week between Porthault sheets in one of the better bedrooms of the American Embassy. Handjobs across the water; no honest hooker ever had it so good, she reflected as the lift shuddered upwards and on-wards to the fifth floor.

She stepped out of her white shoes, wincing, as the lift stopped. Holding them with her suitcase in one hand, the shopping in the other, she padded along the corridor to number thirty-three and let herself in. It was a nice flat; a big living room, a small dining room and two reasonable-sized bed-rooms, kitchen and bathroom. Nice for two, or even three; not so nice for five. Well, four and a half.

She had meant to go straight to the kitchen, but she couldn't resist dumping her bags, shoes and suitcase on the floor and leaning against the locked door for a moment to recover from the journey. She inhaled deeply – and caught the whiff of the food she had stalked in Prague and dragged back to their cave to cook, even through its tightly taped layers of greaseproof wrapping; the acceptable smell of poverty, strong and spicy and making the best of things.

There was Prague ham – *šunka* – *lovecky* salami and six of the long paprika-flavoured sausages called *páreks* – one each, and two for her mother, who was without doubt the head of the house.

Bramborák, the garlic and potato pancakes, she would re-fry on their arrival, and to hell with thoughts of food poisoning. For her sisters, cream cakes ('*Not* German, Ma!'); for her father, six bottles of Budvar; for her mother – the half-Russian, still pro-Soviet Svetlana – Stolichnaya. She loved to get her mother drunk; Svetlana would sing the song of the Volga Boatmen, and swear that Stalin had been 'the man for the job'.

A particularly pungent smell hit the girl, and she sighed as she remembered the disgusting cow's stomach stew – *dršt'ková* – she would have to make in a while. Not have to because she would be beaten if she didn't – but have to because she loved them. And they loved it. But now she was used to eating fillet steak and Scotch salmon at least three times a week, how could she face a floating cow's stomach? (Her own turned over at the thought.)

She'd pretend she was on a diet – she was certainly round enough to get away with it. She pinched both nipples of her big round breasts and they stood to attention immediately. Real professionals, these guys, she thought fondly as she peered down at them; never asleep on the job.

She left her bags and shoes and walked down

the hallway slowly to the room she sometimes shared with her sisters Paulina and Petrova. They were teenagers, thirteen and fifteen; in her day, teenagers as such hadn't really existed. And now these kids had Western desires and Eastern incomes; not good news. A lot of them sold the only thing they had, sex, to bridge the gap between their Disneyland dreams and their drab realities – but not in this house! She walked into the empty, spotless, Spartan room and grinned as she pictured Svetlana drunk, righteous and religious, solemnly swearing to her terrified teenage daughters that if she ever found out – and she had *friends* in the police force, she liked to imply, in Prague – that they had been selling themselves – especially to the Krauts who came over cruising for a bit of exotic Easterner – she would shave their heads. They were both baby blondes, with hair they were racing each other to sit on; this threat had more chance of sticking than any number of moral or religious strictures.

The most beautiful girl in Bohemia loved her father Petre – an incredibly quiet, handsome, soulful man whom she would have married like a shot if she hadn't been his daughter and he hadn't been resident in an Eastern European country; love has *some* limits – but it was the small, stout, sexy, surly Svetlana who was her touchstone. 'She's her mother's daughter!' neighbours would say admiringly when she had kicked yet another local girl or boy (so long as it wasn't theirs) in the crotch for calling Svetlana a dirty Russian.

'Russian, *da*; dirty, *niet*,' she had snarled. Her schoolmates called her Russky until she was thirteen; then, when she became as beautiful as she (or anyone else) would ever be, they just called her – girls to bask in her beauty and pick up excess boys, and boys to – well, why bother? All boys were excess, as far as the most beautiful girl in Bohemia was concerned. For as far back as she could remember, she had set her cold and tired teenage heart on an American.

'There are just two types of men worth giving your virginity to; Russians and Americans,' her mother had told her drunkenly a few months ago. When she had opened her mouth, her mother's face had closed and she held up a hand, palm towards her daughter, blocking any feeble feminine confidences. 'Don't tell me, I don't want to know. Just look after yourself, eh? *Yourself*.'

The room contained bunk beds, and a narrow single; the bunks floated like Lilos among a sea of Keanu Reeves posters, as he smiled down like an Oriental angel through his sleepy safe-sex eyes. On Saturday nights, while their parents innocently watched television game shows next door, Paulina and Petrova would embark on marathon verbal sexual assaults on the young actor, each one outdoing the other with the mounting filthiness of the sexual scenario she most desired. Their elder sister was sure that she hadn't been half so knowing at their ages; still, she'd picked up a few tips while feigning exhausted career-girl sleep.

Her own narrow bed was bordered by two small bedside cabinets her father had knocked together (charmingly Le Corbusier, with those authentic Eastern bloc nails sticking out every which way), one of which held a collection of American self-help psychology and business books (she always kept them after she'd read them, in case a refresher course was called for; all except those dumb women's books like *Women Who Love Too Much*. She couldn't believe anyone would be that stupid, even those bovine American cows; who on earth would be cretinous enough to waste their one and only life on a man who made things worse instead of better? It was flying in the face of Nature! These women should live in Europe East for a season; that would cure them of their moronic masochism).

The other cabinet held a reading lamp, and a strange novelty snowstorm; as tall and smooth as a Perrier bottle, its plastic shell enclosing a grey Statue of Liberty, her face as blank and belligerent as ever. Shake it, and it snowed on her parade.

The young woman took off her black leatherette fake-fur-lined gloves as she walked to her bed. She sat on it, wiggling against its hardness, shook the snowstorm and replaced it on the cabinet, mesmerised like a child. She laughed and clapped her hands as the greying flakes swirled around its head; what an ugly bitch Lady Liberty was! If she could make it there, anyone could!

An old schoolfriend who'd married an American a couple of years ago had sent her the snowstorm; she kept it not for sentimental reasons, as the innocent onlooker might imagine, but for savage ones. Every time she looked at it it reminded her that the point of getting out was not to get just any old American working stiff, but what she thought of as a *real* American; rich, rooted and rolling in it. And now ... she began to breathe quickly and shook the snowstorm again, her narrow eyes narrowing even further.

When she finally got to the Promised Land, she'd send more than tacky snowstorms home! She'd send Levi's, Nintendos, compact discs ... high-heeled leather shoes in every colour of the rainbow. But Martina was a sweet kid; it wasn't really her fault she'd married a plumber from Brooklyn named Mario.

The snowstorm was long and lean, its tip smooth and round. She caressed it absently, still breathing shallowly, and her eyes wandered around the room before stopping at the one and only chair, a cheap and nasty little wicker number. Beneath it, the carpet bulged. But then, it bulged in so many places.

No-one noticed it, under the chair. And if they had, they would have been shocked at the fact that she'd hidden it, not shocked at what it was. It wasn't pornography or a false passport proclaiming her to be a German. She could have stuck it up on this very wall if she'd wanted; it was even more beautiful than Keanu Reeves, just. But she liked to hide it; it made it more ... hers.

She stood up like a sleepwalker and went to the chair. She got down on her hands and knees – Czech foreplay. The carpet was beige and prickly. You can measure whether you're with the right man from the carpet he's laid before you, she thought as she attacked the tacks which held the corner down – because when you kneel for the big blowjob, the pile comes up to your navel. Anything else and you're out of there, little girl, if you know what's good for you.

She gave a final tug and sat back on her heels with her buried treasure revealed in her lap. She unfolded the map once, twice, three, four times; then again, and again. What a big map. What a big country.

'America,' she said softly, as if comforting a sick child. She walked to her sisters' bunks, let a poster flutter to the floor and expropriated its drawing pins. She took them to the wall facing her bed and pinned up the map. Then she stood back and looked at it, squinting very slightly.

'Alabama,' she said thoughtfully, crossing her arms with a hint of criticism. Was it straight? Maybe not exactly – but then, neither would she be.

She went to her bed and plumped up her pillows; went to the bunks and stole her sisters'. She built them all up at the head of the bed and lay down. The view was beautiful – she could see everything. 'Alaska, Arizona, Arkansas,' she said, and smiled luxuriously. She had at least an hour.

'California, Colorado, Connecticut.' The most beautiful girl in Bohemia spoke in measured tones, and pawed vaguely at her breasts. 'Delaware, Florida, Georgia.' Her voice was a fraction faster now, and she grabbed her assets in earnest. 'Hawaii,' she groaned, and pulled open her print dress, tearing a sash at the waist. So what.

'Idaho, Illinois, Iowa,' she gasped. She was clawing at her breasts now, as they leapt from the harness into the hotness. 'Kansas. Kentucky. Louisiana!' She yelped as she drew blood from her bosom, and moaned as the heat between her legs demanded attention ASAP.

'Maine – Maryland – Massachusetts – ' as she rolled her tights and underwear down – 'Michigan, Minnesota, Mississippi – ' as she kicked them on to the floor – 'Missouri, Montana, Nebraska!' in triumph, as her hand went to her clitoris like wildfire. 'New – Hampshire, Jersey, Mexico! New

York, New York! North Carolina, North Dakota!'
She knew now she would never make it to South
Dakota.

Her voice was a rasp now, and her hand entered
her body with the slickness of a doctor's, probing
her cervix. She shrieked with pain but couldn't
stop now. 'Ohio, Oklahoma, Oregon – ' And she
looked around wildly for something to bridge the
gap that suddenly seemed as wide as Texas and as
empty as Wyoming.

She saw the Statue of Liberty snowstorm, and
brought it up, down and up again. Her perineum
rended, but she hardly registered it. She came,
shrieking.

She lay panting, stranded, coming down. 'Penn-
sylvania,' she muttered. 'Rhode Island.' How
come Rhode Island was a state? You never heard
of anyone famous who'd come from there. She fell
to earth and opened her eyes; the room mocked
her, and the map scorned her, and even Keanu
Reeves seemed to look at her with pity. She
looked at the hideous statue snowstorm between
her legs, and yanked it out violently.

The map worked like a charm every time, she admitted to herself as she rolled on to her stomach, still clutching Lady Liberty; she'd never finish the fifty-one states. She looked at the statue, both appalled and amused at herself, and thought what a luxury it was to feel both emotions at once. Then she went to make dinner for her family.

4

Somewhere over Germany, Gary started considering that sooner or later he might get homesick. Landing at Ruzyně Airport, he realised he needn't have worried. Ruzyně was as hideous, overcrowded and inefficient as anything back in dear old Blighty – a right little home from home, and he hadn't even cleared Customs. Yes, any time he got nostalgic he could just catch a cab a few kilometres west from Prague Old Town and get a fix of England in no time.

Dragging his baggage over to the bank of phones, he found the number of Edmond Crichton, the correspondent whose job he was taking – though whether this was with or without his consent was unclear. Cramming the strange currency into the slot, he felt the stab of androidal sexual excitement that comes from being in a new town where no-one knows you.

'Hello?' The middle-aged, upper-crust voice was a yawn which had got ideas above its station, taken a couple of elocution classes and was making a pretty good job of forming words. It was a voice which made Gary think of Russian roulette and untipped cigarettes and losing your job to a young guttersnipe because you were far too jaded and faded to put any passion into it anymore.

'Hello? Is this Edmond Crichton?'

'It is.'

'It's Gary First here. I've arrived.'

'Well, aren't you the lucky one.' The voice sounded amused.

'No, the thing is, I'm at the airport. And I wondered, if it's not any trouble, if we could organise a meet as soon as possible. I'm afraid I don't know the first thing about Prague.' This obviously wasn't true, after Stewart's cruel and unusual punishment, but it was a way to make the sad old guy feel useful.

'Well, I can recommend a very good guide book, written in the style of the younger set if you find Fodor rather heavy going. It's a Cadogan City Guide, written by – '

'I've read all the books,' Gary blurted. 'What I need from you isn't information, it's your *take* on this place. It's like your fingerprints – you've got the only one of its kind. Look, please meet me just this once – I'm a fast learner, and I won't be asking you to be pen pals. All I need is thirty minutes of your life. What do you say?'

There was a silence, then a sigh; Gary could almost hear him tucking in his shirt and straightening his tie. 'OK, motormouth – you've got yourself a blind date. Or do I mean a blind drunk? Whatever, meet me at a café called the Slavia, on Národní, opposite the National Theatre. Do you want to drop your bags off first?'

'Yeah! thanks, Mr Crichton, you won't regret this.'

'I doubt that. But I'll see you there in an hour. There. Better?'

'Brilliant! Bye!'

His bags when he picked them up felt as though they had been emptied entirely of their contents, and he didn't care. And his heart felt even lighter as he made his way out to the taxi rank.

Bending down to the front window, he tapped on the glass. The driver looked up from his paper, lips still moving from reading the *Sun*.

It was Edmond Crichton who had so thoughtfully semaphored his liking for the lush, but it was Gary First who arrived at the Slavia Café feeling drunk – punch-drunk with the sinister beauty of Prague. With its mass of domes and spires, its bent bridges and clocks that moved backwards, it was like entering a game of Dungeons and Dragons designed by Disney from a rough sketch by Kafka.

It was like no city he had ever seen; he kept expecting the curtain with this Baroque beauty oil-painted on to it to rise and reveal the ram-shackle stage-set beyond. But it hadn't during the ride from Ruzyně to the flat on Malá Strana, and it didn't as he walked up to the Slavia.

It was a large, shabby café, half full on this

working day. Self-consciously, Gary went to the counter and spoke his first words of Czech to a native. As luck would have it, his cabbie had been a lecherous Anglophile who spoke perfect *Sun*-English and quizzed Gary about his knowledge – carnal or otherwise – of such 'stunnas' as Kathy Lloyd and Suzanne Mizzi.

'*Káva, prosím.*'

The surly bartender didn't miss a beat. 'Double? With milk chaser?'

Suitably smarting from the global scolding, Gary took his cup to a corner table, sat down and debated with himself whether or not to open the copy of *The European* he was rather self-regardingly carrying. Would it look too unbearably naff and smug? And anyway, it was such a lousy paper, though a great idea. How beautiful the words were – our common European home. *Very* common, come to think of it – they all seemed to be *Sun* readers. Maybe the fact that the *Sun* was twenty times better written and designed than *The European* had something to do with it – or maybe they just liked the 'stunnas'. Either way, he compromised by displaying *The European* prominently on the table; there was far more to absorb him in the view of Národní Avenue.

Through the window a man who used to be handsome stopped and stared at Gary, then smiled. Instantly Gary knew it must be Edmond Crichton. Around fifty, he was obviously a good way into a long-term project which consisted of turning both to drink and to seed. Even the meanest form teacher would have given him a B+ for effort. His clothes were well cut, but almost audibly fraying. In another profession he would have been regarded as one of their distressed gentlefolk, and in the old, smug world of journalism as a revered 'character' – which sounded good, but in the end meant you got treated as precisely that; a *character*, not quite a real person.

But in the journalistic world of today, Edmond was just another old lush – the sort of could-have-been-a-contender cliché that boys such as Gary found cringe-making.

Gary watched him walk on, come through the door of the Slavia and cross to his table. He stood up; Edmond held out a plump pink hand that hid a killer grip. Gary winced and Edmond laughed.

'My body is a deadly weapon. You must be Gary First.'

Gary dropped into a chair, nursing his hand. 'Did they send you a photo?'

Edmond looked at him with amused calculation, and signalled for a waiter who not only materialised instantly but mutated from brooding poet to twinkling maitre d'.

'*Burčak*, dear heart,' said Edmond.

'What's that?' asked Gary as the waiter went to get it.

'The first Czech wine of the year – a sort of semi-fermented Beauj Nouv. Tastes like Ribena, then knocks you for six. Or seven.' He took it from the waiter, and raised it towards Gary. 'Cheers. What's that you're drinking?'

'Coffee,' said Gary resignedly.

'Double?' Edmond smirked.

'With milk chaser,' Gary finished sullenly. 'So how did you recognise me?'

'By your bloom, dear boy.'

'The bloom of youth, you mean?' Gary was fast getting hip to Edmond's sexual preference, and it made him a mite uneasy.

'Hardly.' Edmond drank. 'No, I was referring to the bloom of the West.'

'What's that like, when it's at home?' Gary relaxed.

53

'It's a sort of shine. Or is it sheen? I never know the difference. But it comes from being accustomed to choosing from twenty brands of shampoo.' Edmond shrugged. 'Whatever, you'll have lost it after six weeks east of the Elbe.' He drained his glass and signalled for another. 'In fact, I'll bet you hard cash right now that within the month you'll have gone native. You'll be wearing plastic shoes and slapping talc in your passion pits in lieu of deodorant. Can't be helped. It's hard going keeping a shine on your shoes when you're wading knee-deep through a sewer.'

Gary laughed incredulously, and gestured through the window at Národní Avenue. 'A sewer! You need your eyes testing!'

Edmond looked through the window and nodded thoughtfully. 'Yes, it's pretty enough. But then, you can always put a quilted satinette cover on a toilet roll. That doesn't stop it from being a bloody toilet roll.'

Gary could feel the tension snake through his body; his first day in the city, and he was already half in love with it. 'Then I take it you'll be glad to be going back to dear old Blighty.'

'Listen.' Edmond received his second drink,

and it made him conciliatory. 'I'm not political. No foreign correspondent can afford to be, unless he's really got his heart set on going home in a bucket.' He drank. 'But over the past five years, I've come to the reluctant conclusion that Communism was but the tourniquet some clever brutes put on this part of the world to keep the top on it.'

'Really? How so?' Gary drawled, looking like someone who knew all the answers. Edmond looked at him sharply, and Gary realised he had tried to make fun before he could walk.

'Oh, come *on*.' Edmond's voice oozed sarcasm. 'You don't *really* want to hear my opinion of this place, now do you? Because basically I'm just a burnt-out, boozed-up, jacked-in, broken-down old failure, bitter because he's leaving the Prague posting with just as indifferent a career as he came to it with, aren't I? And a poof to boot.' He laughed wearily into Gary's startled face. 'I can read you like a book, little boy. And you've underlined all the obvious clichés and mistaken them for piercing insights, and you've written prissy little notations in the margins, just like the conscientious, upwardly mobile little prig you are.' He stood up. 'Forget it. You've come here believing, oh, let me see, that the people of Eastern Europe – and none more so than the plucky little Czechs! – are a proud, valiant race of poet-warriors to whom liberty is even more important than bread. And who – once the corrupting, crippling yoke of Communism is lifted from their blemish-free backs – will soar up straight as an arrow from capitalism's quiver into the wide blue horizon of limitless possibilities. Taking tired old Western Europe with them, no doubt, on target for a brave new pan-European renaissance.' He leaned down, put his plush paws on the table and narrowed his eyes at Gary. With one finger he tapped the copy of *The European* with brilliant disdain. 'You've read all about it. What on earth could I tell you? I've only been here half a decade.' He dropped some stray *haler* coins on the table, and turned to go.

Jumping up, Gary grabbed his arm. He could not believe he felt such panic at a stranger's intention to leave a café, both of which he hardly knew.

'No! Please don't go!'

Edmond turned back and looked at his face,

then at his hand. His gaze stayed there. 'Unhand me. Or I'll shake your hand again.'

Gary let go. 'I'm sorry – *I'm sorry*. If in any way I indicated that I thought you had nothing to teach me, I apologise completely. Please sit down – I'll get you another drink.'

Edmond shot him a poison look.

'*A* drink. OK?'

'*Slivovice*. Double.' Edmond sat down warily, as much on the edge of his chair as his bulky body would allow, and looked combatively at Gary.

Gary kept his eyes fixed on Edmond's, as though this could freeze him to the spot. He didn't move as the waiter came up at a trot. '*Slivovice*. Doubles. Two of them.' As the waiter left, Gary leaned forward beseechingly. 'Please – tell me what you know. I need a handle on this city – this *country*. *Now*. I don't want to stumble around like a greenhorn for months on end looking for clues – I want to start straight away. So I need your take on Czechoslovakia, desperately. The D-Notice take.'

Edmond smiled at the waiter, who placed before him a double *slivovice* – at least twice as large as the one he placed before Gary – lit a cigarette, drank, and looked at him before staring out at Národní. Then he sighed, and shook his head. He smiled wryly at Gary, and leaned forward. Their foreheads almost touching, Edmond spoke fast and low.

'OK. Here's what I've come to think about this country. Or rather, its people – because Czechoslovakia *is* its people; like England, but not like France or America. And the people are charming – just like the view you see beyond that window, and defend with such zeal after only an hour here. But they're also savage, and they can be dangerous. Like this city itself.'

'Go on.'

'This is Boom Town – without the boom. The Gold Rush – without the gold. It's Dodge City – with AIDS and Nazis. And not just here – it's the whole of Godforsaken, disinherited, freefalling Eastern Europe. Here, at least it's beautiful.

'The people here are hungry – not for food, but for the Promised Land they believed was waiting for them at the end of the Communist rainbow. And unlike your real starving, your Third Worlders, they're dangerous because they're angry – and so close to home. They're angry because they believe they've been done out of their birth-right.'

Gary was fascinated. 'What birthright?'

Edmond smiled slyly. 'The one they were meant to get for being *white*, of course. *White Europeans* – the architects of civilisation! Pass Go, collect £200 sterling and a Sony Walkman.' He drank from his glass of plum brandy. 'Pigment really means something to these people, you see – they're like Mississippi white trash. Being pallid's all they have to be proud of – all that distinguishes them from the rest of the world's beggars. With their noses pressed up against the windows of the West. And then they hear all this fancy politico talk about a New World Order. A common European home – with no frontiers! And for them, it's the green light – mass jailbreak. They're bitter, these people, and it's the sort of bitterness you see in men who've spent twenty years pleasuring Her Majesty. They feel they're being punished for something they didn't do. And you bet they're sore, as the cousins say.

'So there they are – revving up for their day in the sun; their rush around the hypermarket with the wire trolley, cramming in as much as they can in the ten minutes of hog heaven at the end of the game show. Come on down, Czechoslovakia – it's your turn!'

'And then?' asked Gary humbly. A trifle too humbly; Edmond looked at him sharply, then re-relaxed.

'And then, when they get there – too late. The cupboard, it would seem, is bare; the party's over. They got the date wrong, and now there's something called a *recession*. And *Green politics*. Which means that not only is it a damn sight harder to enjoy yourself than it used to be – it's also *morally wrong*. And when they get there, to the gardens of the West, even the Krauts – the *Krauts*! – look at them as if they're black. Common European home? They're treated like trespassers on some great estate.

'So no-one here believes in anything any more; everyone's on the take, on the make. It's Darwinian capitalism in the raw; makes New York look community-minded. If a girl's decent-looking, nine times out of ten she's a whore – whether money changes hands or not. If a man's clever, he's got a racket running. Whatever, they're looking after numero uno twenty-four hours a day.

That leaves precious little time for rebuilding the beloved country.' He drained his *slivovice* and looked around for more.

'Waiter!'

'But I don't want you to think I've been unhappy here. Good God, no. In many ways, this state of affairs makes it a very comfy little patch indeed for a man like myself to eke out his decadent decline in. If a beautiful young man is hungry for learning, if he wants to know which wine goes with which cut of black-market meat, or which knife to stick into the roving hand of the foreign fat-cat correspondent, who am I to withhold such knowledge?' Edmond sighed deeply into his fresh drink. 'The only trouble is that not a lot of them *are* beautiful; it's the teeth, I'm afraid. For anyone brought up on a VistaVision diet of all-American sparklers, Eastern European teeth do *not* cut the Colman's. Like the geisha with her blackened stumps, they're beautiful until they smile.' He smiled himself. 'Unfortunately, unlike the geisha, they don't have the wit to cover the yawning chasms with their hands. Very unappetising.'

There was a desperate silence, and Gary felt his

ears turn red. He knew there was nothing wrong with homosexuality. In fact, when it was between two consenting women wearing nice underwear and being filmed, he was all in favour. But he was buggered if he could sincerely sympathise with a raddled old brownie-hound about the orthodontically challenged Middle European male. It would just sound phoney.

'What are the women like?' he blurted.

Edmond shrugged, profoundly uninterested.'The Thais of Mitteleuropa. Or so I hear.' He smiled warmly and briefly over Gary's shoulder through the window, raising his hand in greeting. 'See for yourself.'

Coming through the doorway of the Slavia Café was the most beautiful woman Gary had ever seen. She was that strange and rare thing – a blonde with class, a blonde who was not a blonde in anything but pigmentation. Her hair was almost yellow and fell to the top of her breasts – but her regal way of moving, her savage, slanted, Slavic face and expression of disapproving aloofness could not have been less 'blonde', if blonde has become a shorthand for vacuousness, vulgarity and a desire to pander to the lowest desires of men. Built like a ballerina who had taken vows of silicone and run away to join a pony show, she was perfectly tall, scarily pale and basically filthy. She was wonderful.

Gary's heart went AWOL in that moment; it was aiming for his mouth, but took a wrong turning on a one-way street and ended up in his groin instead. It figured it may as well take a rest there, and settled down to enjoy the view as the beauty crossed to the counter. She said something to the barman, pulled out and lit herself a cigarette with a box of matches – Gary was shocked to find himself shocked by the fact that here a beautiful woman did not have a beautiful cigarette lighter ; for crying out loud, you've become quite pathetically bourgeoise, he scolded himself – and opened a book – *The Art of the Deal* by Donald Trump – while she waited.

'Who's that?' Gary whispered, transfixed.

'Maria Vachss.' Edmond, the narky old ginger, was mocking him by answering in a saccharine approximation of his awed, slo-mo whisper.

'What does she do?' The mating call of the Eighties.

'She's a freelance translator – works for

publishers, the embassies. Even – are you sitting down, dear boy? – for us.'

'Is she smart?' The politically correct mating call of the Nineties.

'*I'll* say,' leered Edmond. 'Not too hard on the eye, either. No?'

'She's *beautiful*.'

'She's *taken*.'

Maria was taking her glass from the barman, closing her book, sliding off her stool, coming their way.

Gary made his voice even softer. 'Animal, vege-table or millionaire?'

Maria was passing their table looking directly ahead of her. As she drew level with them she spoke, in beautiful, high, clear, musical English, 'Millionaire. Also, she speaks extremely good English. And has *exceptionally* good hearing.' She put her glass and book on their table leaned across to Gary and smiled like a shiv. 'And no, she *isn't* in the habit of getting herself up in suspenders and a bowler hat and crouching on a looking-glass for your pleasure. Lena Olin. A *Swede*.'

His mouth, somehow, had found itself slightly open; with one delicate gesture, her right forefinger pushed up his jaw. It clicked.

'Don't *drool*, gringo,' she said with another wicked smile before picking up her things and moving on.

Edmond laughed and raised his empty glass. 'Welcome to Prague!'

5

In his tiny office in the BBC building, Gary sat staring at the map of the world on the opposite wall. Maps of the world always had the effect of making him feel both euphoric and sorrowful at the same time – euphoric at his future, sorrowful at its past – which in turn made him feel confused. As he'd arrived at work already feeling all three of these things, staring at the map could have been seen as wallowing. But he couldn't keep his eyes away.

Making a real effort, he wrenched his eyes to the essential accessories in the classic tableau of the writer who can't write; the cornucopia of stationery – so called, no doubt, because there was no way it was going to be *moving*. Yes, there was precious little meat or motion in store for the piles of lined and unlined A4, the yellow legal pads, the graph paper, the scratch paper, the recycled blocks of multi-coloured paper. Or for the pens; a rainbow of ballpoint and felt-tip, ranging from the chunkiest Dayglo marker to the soberest, finest nylon nib. His nibs! Gary thought grimly, and not a nibble in sight.

One of the small army of pencils seemed less capable of GBH than the others; sensing a challenge, Gary grabbed his sharpener and honed it until the point fell off. That seemed pretty much to sum up his working week so far; embarrassing enthusiasm completely losing its point after three days of lukewarm introductions to totally uninterested Czech and English colleagues whose only words of advice were more like words of warning. 'Listen, one thing you've got to remember; only the killer stories from Eastern Europe get airtime. And most of *those* come from the AKA' (shorthand for whatever the once and future Soviet Union was calling itself this week).

Gary looked at his watch. She was late. His hands, working with a mind of their own – obviously they'd borrowed the one intended for his head – rearranged the pencils to make a capital letter M. He sighed, brushed back the glossy brown hair from his forehead, and dislodged a contact lens.

He was under the desk, scouring the regulation STD clinic carpet, when the door opened and he saw a pair of cheap, white, high-heeled shoes. Growing out of them, all the way to heaven, were slender curved legs in sheer tights as dark as brown could be without turning black. The paleness of her skin shone through them, giving them the look of Lycra. She came down to his level, with a crooked and superior smile. Her hair was back in a barrette, and she wore bright red matte lipstick with no rouge or eye make-up. She wore a dark green jersey dress with a high neck and buttoned cuffs. Perhaps the shoes were lucky or something.

Maria dabbed her finger to the carpet and held it out to him, in front of his dazed, mismatched eyes. 'You're looking for this?'

'Cheers.' He grabbed it gracelessly, stumbled backwards and upwards on to his chair and attempted to hide his embarrassment in his contact lens case.

'Do you have the solution?' she asked innocently, enjoying her poise.

'Very funny.' He was whole again. He snapped the drawer shut and looked at his watch triumphantly. 'You're late.'

'You're running on Czech time now; half an hour late for everything. I'm only ten minutes late. Which means I'm early.' Walking around the desk, she peered at the M and smiled. 'So. I understand you need some help. Shall we start?'

Cursing himself silently, Gary scattered the M and handed her a report. 'I was having a bit of aggro with this.'

She climbed on to his desk and sat with her back to him, her waist level with his mouth. Her dress had tiny green buttons all the way down the back.

'Yes?' She studied it. 'You read Czech?'

'A bit. I'm still learning.'

'It's a good language, as they go; relatively easy to learn. Not a knees-together pig like Polish. It's phonetic, with no nonsense about silent letters like you have.' She swivelled and smiled. 'So much silence in your language, yes?'

'Yeah.'

She turned back to it. 'Though sadly, our language has given only two words to yours, unless you count Semtex. And they are "Pistol" and "robot." '

'How very appropriate.'

'Why so?' She didn't turn.

'Since you're a perfect blend of both.'

She laughed throatily, as though gargling with body fluids. 'Those who know me know better. Ah! – now I see why you couldn't decipher this – it's not actually in Czech at all. It's in Bureaucratese – I can hardly make sense of it myself. Stop looking at me like that.' She didn't miss a beat.

Stunned, Gary opened his mouth to protest. Then he laughed, amazed and amused. 'How did you know?'

'Act your age, Mr First. Of *course* you were casing me. Also, there was a considerable draught on my back; in your mind's eye, you were popping those buttons like crazy.'

He was quiet, then he said resentfully, 'You're very sure of yourself.'

She swivelled round and leaned down; she was very near, looking him straight in the eye, and he could smell her slightly off, slightly metallic breath. The contrast with her dreamgirl beauty was almost obscene – in a *good* way – and made her even more appealing, far more than a bland waft of regulation mint synthetic would have. It was as though smelling her real mouth was in some way one step towards smelling the realness of the rest of her. And already, he couldn't imagine anything better. Except promotion.

She didn't touch him, but he felt as though he was being held tight by the shoulders as she said, urgently yet slowly, 'When you're not sure of anything else in this world, you'd better be sure of yourself.'

'Will you have lunch with me?' Swept away, he spoke as urgently as she did. As soon as the line was out it struck him that the emphasis wasn't perhaps equally necessary.

Obviously she thought so too. Throwing back her head so fiercely that the barrette fell to the floor and her hair fell down over her face and shoulders – in slow motion, it seemed to Gary – she laughed a laugh that seemed masculine in its

72

strength and cruelty. She looked utterly beautiful and merciless. And when the rubble cleared, she said, still smiling, 'Now why would I want to do a thing like that?'

Bitch! Just in time, he pulled himself together and tried a late volley of sarcasm. 'Sorry. I realise I'm not in your league.'

'Damn right.' She eased herself off the desk, smoothing her dress with one hand and shaking the document at him with the other. 'I'll take this junk away and decode it for you.' Ambling to the door, she stopped, pulled a pen from her sleeve, wrote something on the protective top sheet, amazingly made it into a perfect paper plane and flew it serenely straight to his lap. 'And I'll meet you there. We'll make love, I think.'

He looked at her, speechless once more.

'At seven o'clock. Don't be late. You'll know me – I'll be the exotic Easterner wearing the sardonic smile and the cheap white shoes.' She smiled at him with what seemed like genuine liking, seemed about to say something – and walked through the door, closing it quietly behind her.

In the beautiful, decaying Art Nouveau Hotel Evropa in the centre of Wenceslas Square, Gary glanced at his watch. It was a quarter to eight and, whether you were on Greenwich Mean Time, British Summer Time or Prague Screw-Up Time, she was late in anyone's language. Too late.

He finished his bad martini – sickly sweet vermouth which had merely had 'gin' whispered to it – and looked around the bar at the groups of unappetising Western businessmen carousing determinedly with flashily – some would say trashily – dressed Czech women. White stilettoes were obviously à la mode here. He found them all slightly disgusting, but perhaps he was only jealous. The thought disturbed him, and he dropped a handful of *halér* on the table and got up to go.

As he walked through the lobby, a small dark girl in a uniform of dove grey and white approached him. She stood in front of him, and looked at him querulously.

'I left your tip – *tip, halér* – on the table,' he pantomimed at her.

'You are Mr First, yes?'

'Yes,' he agreed suspiciously.

'Come to meet Maria Vachss?'

74

'Yes.' Surprised wasn't in it.

She smiled, a brunette's secret smile so different from the blonde's extrovert beacon. 'Come with me, please.'

He followed her back through the lobby and up the stairs, being careful of the rickety banisters, through the open lobby on the second floor with the skylight three floors above, to a room at the end of the corridor. She stopped in front of it and smiled at him over her shoulder. Then she tapped lightly on the door three times and turned a key from the bunch on her hip in the lock.

The door swung open, she smiled at him one last time and padded away silently. He pushed the door, entered the room and closed it behind him. Something told him that whatever lay behind the door had to be kept a secret.

The room was less a room than four walls built around a four-poster bed. At each corner, a candle provided the room's only light. Except that which radiated from Maria, who lay in the bed. Black velvet bands bound her wrists to the upper posts, and there was an identical band around her neck. Her shoulders were bare above the sheets.

'You're late. On Czech time, already?'

He didn't move. 'I thought … the bar … '

'You thought I would hang around in bars like a cheap *prostitute*?' She laughed throatily and wriggled in her bonds. 'What sort of girl do you think I *am*?'

'Are you real?'

'As real as you are, Mr First.'

As if by pre-arranged agreement, the candles burned out.

He went forward and stumbled; he fell on the bed and groped for her. But it was empty; how had she slipped her bonds? 'Where are you?' he whispered stupidly.

'Here.'

'Where?'

'Right in the front of you! Can't you smell me, Mr First? I'm on heat.' She laughed, nastily; he realised he was in the presence of what Marco, the authority, called a Nasty Girl.

('What's a Nasty Girl, then?' 'Well – it's a slag, basically. A girl what goes. *Only* – ' and here Marco held up a stubby son-of-the-Sicilian-soil finger, which had incidentally never done an honest day's work in its life ' – you *respect* her. Don't ask me why. But that's what a Nasty Girl is.

76

You'll know her when you meet her.')

Gary stopped, and sniffed. He must look like a randy mutant rabbit, he reflected. But it paid off; the musky, mulchy smell came from a certain corner. He stumbled towards it, brushed a fantastic pair of bazooms with a blundering hand, and felt her move swiftly away.

'What game do you call this?' He tried hard to make his voice sound urbane and amused, but he was only too aware that he simply sounded like a silly little man who couldn't get his end away.

'Blind man in the buff,' she said.

Gary stopped stock still and, with the skill of one who deals in voices, analysed hers. It was teasing, yes, but it did not have the shallow smugness of the tease proper, pure and simple. There was a raw note beneath it; jagged and troublesome, like a ragged nail snagging a silk stocking. She really might be, he realised, on heat.

'Blind man's bluff,' he said softly, and smiled almost audibly. He stayed still, and in the dark began to stroke his cock, pulling the shaft back and forth over the circumcised head. It was a beauty, big and smooth and shining healthy baby pink, even if he had to say it this time himself –

which he usually didn't. In his mind's eye a hundred girls (well, thirty) rose up like Tiller Girls and chorused 'It's *gorgeous!* Are you *sure* you're not Jewish?' Truth to tell, he'd been mistaken for a Jewish baby called Greville First at the hospital where he was born and done before him and instead of him; more than two decades later it was still paying dividends. He tried to make it make a sticky noise; it wouldn't. Clean as a whistle. (Were whistles clean?) He laughed.

'What are you doing?' Her voice was weird, foreign, new; she'd dropped her baton. And he'd picked it up, and was jerking it off.

'Come on, Maria – you're the one with the extra-sensory lugholes, aintcha?'

'What is lugholes? And what do you do? Why you laugh?'

'Puuure ... pleasuuure.' He stroked the words top to tail, like a cat. 'Can't you smell me, Miss Vachss? I'm wanking.'

'What ... ?' She was panicking. She was the stranger, not he, in a strange land. 'Why? ... what do you do for?'

'I thought you wanted to play, Maria? See – I'll play with you.' He chuckled, trying to be a Nasty

Boy and failing, he thought. 'I hear you're losing your English. But this is an international language – no?'

'No.' She was stolidly accepting her confusion; beauty at bay, but not quite beat. 'Let me ... give me ... ' He heard her blunder into a piece of dumb furniture, something he wouldn't have dreamed physically possible this morning from seeing her clothed; she swore, in Czech. She was losing it. 'Gary?'

'Right here,' he said pseudo-soothingly. 'Right here, and as hard as your heart. Come and get it, if you want it – before it's gone.'

He heard her lurch desperately towards his voice, and ducked away into a corner. 'Move it, darling – I can feel something stirring down here. Something *seminal*. This is it – last offer, never repeated. Come – '

The door suddenly opened, and a beautiful, nude Fuzzy Felt silhouette of a woman slipped out of his life. He couldn't believe it. He'd blown it – or rather, wanked it. Right into an empty bed. He dropped the baton himself, totally totalled. 'Maria?' he said pathetically, going towards the door.

He saw too late, but beautifully, that the door was not closed but ajar; it opened with a fluorescent flash of corridor and the most fearless girl he had ever met jumped into the room as though it were a swimming pool – the deep end – with a triumphant peal of laughter that sounded like the biggest splash he had ever heard.

In the light she brought behind her he was a standing, naked target; she leaped on to him and pushed him, still carrying her, backwards on to the bed. Her legs were around his waist, her arms around his neck and her hands around his heart. She squeezed, ever so slightly, and he gasped as he slid up into her.

She leaned down to whisper, stooped to conquer with a caress. It was a fact; she had won. He had never felt so vulnerable – or so victorious.

'You'd better be good, after all this,' she hissed. 'Because if you're not, I'm going to slice off your dick while it's still inside me and serve it up to my family on Saturday night. We eat anything here, you know.'

The spark from the smallest of guns split their

darkness. It was Maria's new lighter, in the shape of a pistol, shooting a stream of flame from which she lit two cigarettes. She handed one to Gary. He was propped up on one elbow, staring at her.

'There's a joke,' she said, placing an ashtray between them. 'Why do Czechs sleep with Westerners?' She got up and moved to the window, pulling up the blind. Street lights lit the room softly. In the West, you could pay some interior decorating poove thousands for lighting like that. Or maybe she'd just look good in anything. 'Answer; for the cigarette afterwards.' She went back to the bed and sat opposite him. 'Marlboro. Craven A. Consulate. Do you know how beautiful those words were to me when I was growing up?' She laughed unpleasantly, as though at the memory of her teenage self. 'Can you imagine finding the word "Camel" glamorous?'

Her mood affected his. 'Is that why you slept with me?' he said chippily. 'For the cigarette afterwards?'

'I should probably slap your face for that. But I'll let it go, as you're obviously suffering from a bad case of post-coital triste. Any other women's trouble? Do you get period pains, too?'

'I'm sorry.' He looked down at the bed. 'This is

a one-off for you, isn't it? You're not going to see me again.'

She was silent.

'Why?' He tried to make it sound interested and impartial. Not a plea. But she still didn't answer. So he thought he might as well plead. 'Just tell me why, will you? Was it something I did?'

She put out her hand and held his chin. 'Haven't you ever slept with someone just once, Gary?' Her voice was very soft, but not particularly kind; soft cop, with hard cop standing by.

'No!' Lying bastard. 'Yes... .'

'It's very safe, just doing it once.' She sounded as though she was talking to herself. 'It almost doesn't count as sex at all. It's more like an accident, no? And accidents will happen, isn't that what you say?'

'That wasn't an accident. That was a massacre.' He grabbed her suddenly by the shoulders. 'I've got to see you again. It's not that I want to. It's that I've *got* to.'

She shook him off and looked at him warily. Then calculatingly. She took a drag on her cigarette and hissed it out. Then she spoke. 'OK, Gary. All right. But you've got to make me a promise, and you've got to keep it.'

'Anything.' He meant it. At that moment.

'You mustn't fall in love with me. Or me with you. If you do, or if I do, we must finish. No arguments, no analysis, no blame – as though the other one had died. Understand?'

'Right!' he said eagerly. Then, 'Why?'

'I'm engaged to be married.' She put out her cigarette. 'Didn't Edmond tell you, in the Slavia?'

'He said you were "taken". I just thought you were … I don't know. Going out with someone.'

'No, I'm engaged. It was in the American newspapers – the works. He's with the US Embassy – goes back in six weeks. I'm going with him.'

'I see.'

'So it wouldn't be a good idea to fall in love. You've got to stay here, for your career – I've got to leave here, for my sanity. For six weeks we can have fun. But we can't fall in love.'

'Sure. What's he like?'

'LaMonte? He's very nice.'

'Rich? Sorry – stupid question.'

She shrugged. 'It's as easy to love a rich man as a poor one. Yes, he's quite wealthy – his family is well established in Washington. He doesn't need to work, I guess. But he's interested in this part of

Europe; its oldness, its rawness. I think it excites him, coming from such a new, clean country.'

'Do you sleep with him?' Gary sulked.

'No, we read the *Wall Street Journal* to each other.'

'Is he good?'

She didn't answer.

'*Is* he?'

'He's not like you. Satisfied?' She shivered, hugging herself.

Again he grabbed her. 'Is he bad to you?'

'I don't want to talk about it. But *you're* hurting me, if that's what you mean to do.'

'Sorry.' He let go. 'Does he – do anything to you you don't want him to do? You know what I mean.'

She shook her head. 'It's not that. Not what you're thinking.' She bit her lip, and then blurted, 'He just likes me to lie very still, and look sad. To cry sometimes. And then he'll say, "My poor little girl! My poor little peasant! Don't cry – I'll rescue you. Uncle's here!" '

There was a ghastly silence for a moment as they gaped at each other, stunned at how sexually crass Americans could be. Then Gary burst into raucous laughter.

'What is so funny?' demanded Maria angrily.

'You!' Gary hooted. 'That vision of you – as a poor little peasant girl – waiting to be rescued by Uncle. Uncle!' He collapsed, insensible.

'Go on – mock me,' Maria spat resentfully. 'I bloody hate it, actually, if you want to know.'

He was suddenly serious. He'd been allowed to get his metaphorical foot in the door. 'Then why do it?'

'I have to get to America.' She could not be moved, just like in the song. Stubborn as a meritocratic mule. 'You could never understand.'

How far had they gone tonight? A bit too bloody far, in her case, Gary thought now. 'I can't understand *ambition*? That's a good one. Remind me to tell you something about myself some time, when we're not fucking each other's brains out.'

'Which in your case would take all of two minutes.' She smiled hesitantly at him.

'Ha bloody ha.' He stroked her hair; despite its sheen, its texture was resilient, almost rough, more like straightened Afro-Caribbean hair than the silkiness of the Caucasian cliché. 'You can get there. And you can get there as *yourself*. You're good at your job – and every country needs translators, especially now with the world opening up the way it is. Anywhere you want to get, you can get there by yourself.'

She snorted. 'Which fortune cookie did you get *that* one out of?'

He knew it had been a stupid thing to say; here he was trying to wow her with English sang-froid, and he'd started talking like her bloody fiancé. But he toughed it out. 'Cliché or not, it's true.'

'As a *career girl* I'm meant to go to the West?' Her voice was contemptuous; of career girls, of him, of all the stupid world, especially the soft, stupid West. 'And share a crummy little flat with two stewardesses who hang their douche bags behind the bathroom door? No thanks.'

'It doesn't have to be like that – '

'Not for you, maybe. But for me it would. I've heard about the price of apartments and the pitiful few square feet you get over there. I have that already, thank you. And I think I would prefer to share a bedroom with two small sisters whose personal habits are well known to me than with two raddled American strangers who probably have body-positive brassieres.' She sighed impatiently and lit another cigarette. 'I'm not *looking* for a home from home – I need to be *rich*. And I'm sorry if that sounds bad, but I don't care; there are some people born to dance, or run, or climb mountains, and some who are born to be rich. I'm one of them.' She looked at him fiercely. 'Anyway – if I were to break my engagement. Work for a living. In London. Would you leave Prague?'

She had him. He opened his mouth to flannel her, then stopped. 'I can't. Not for two years. I'd never get another job in broadcasting if I threw in the towel now. It'd be back to the Street of Shame with my CV between my legs.'

'You see?' She smoked definitively. 'It's hopeless.'

They sat in silence for a minute. Then he said, 'That little bird who brought me up here – who was she?' Anything to break the silence that swamped them.

'Katya,' she answered moodily, but with a slight lightening of tone. 'My friend from school. I told her to look out for you.' She smiled at him, still friends. 'To bar your way bodily if you tried to leave without fucking me.'

He laughed, relieved; he was starting to realise that he liked her more than any girl he'd ever

87

known. A girl who didn't want to fall in love! Flesh of his flesh. 'How did you describe me to her?'

She paused. Then said slowly, 'I'm not going to tell you.'

'Go on.' He was fascinated now.

'No! It's private!'

He grabbed her and rolled her on to her back, holding her wrists down. 'Tell me! Or I'll make you say "Uncle!" '

She was laughing, looking as though she didn't have a care in the world. 'Please! Anything but that!' She straightened her face with an effort. 'OK. You win. I said you were – ' She turned her face away, then began to laugh again. She spat it into his face with her laughter, '*Divocak!*'

'Divo-*what?*'

'*Divocak!*' She was off again. 'It means wild pig! It also means sex on legs!' She was suddenly serious, looking him straight in the eye. 'All three of them,' she said sternly.

He weakened, and in that moment she saw her chance and pushed him backwards, reversing their positions. She had a silky, steely streamlined strength, like an Eastern Bloc gymnast. He was helpless; her hair fell over his face, and her grip was unbelievable. She made Marco look like a mincing ginger.

'Open your mouth,' she ordered.

Powerless to resist, he did so. To his surprise, she spat into it with all her might. He got a mouthful.

'Now you belong to me,' she told him as he blinked moistly at her. Then she kissed him savagely, biting his lips until they bled, and they made love for the fourth time that night. Yet again, Gary wondered why they called it 'casual' sex.

6

Gary walked into the BBC canteen, his mood greyer than the steel serving hatches. Without looking at the alleged food available, he went straight to a table and sat down next to Alexander, a sparky young Czech journo he'd exchanged Western fashion tips with a few times in corridors. Like a right bastard he'd told Alexander that it was still dead hip to roll up the sleeves of your jacket, and the poor sap was walking around like a refugee from *Miami Vice*.

Alexander looked up chuckling from his *Viz*, no doubt anticipating a bit of raw British humour in the flesh. He was sorely disappointed.

'Cheer up. It might never happen, no?'

'Too right it might not ever bloody happen!' Gary lit a cigarette and instantly thought of Maria. What was she up to now? Having her post-coital Camel, or sitting on her fiancé's face? He had to stop thinking about her, especially with his brilliant new career careening up Crap Creek at a rate of knots. 'Not if my superiors in their ruddy wisdom have anything to do with it!'

'Another no?' Alexander was sympathetic.

'Another *niet*, more like. You know the drill. "Young man, the BBC can only devote a certain number of hours per week to the depressing mess Eastern Europe has become. And it so happens that we find the squabbling of what used to be the Soviet Union considerably more interesting than what width of gold braid the Prague Palace Guard have on their uniforms this week." '

'And that's the third story they've turned down, the braid one?'

'Do me a favour, Alex!' Gary was indignant. 'Of course I didn't turn in a story about bloody braid.

Give me some credit!'

'Gary, I'm prepared to give you all the credits you want,' said Alexander gently. 'It's your bosses who seem reluctant.'

'Sorry. I asked for that.' Gary fell silent, sick of the sound of his own moaning voice.

'What was it this time, then?' asked Alexander after a minute.

'The growing plight of Prague's buskers,' Gary answered reluctantly.

Alexander nodded solemnly. Then tea splattered from his mouth as he choked with laughter.

'OK! I know I need a hot story. But they don't grow on trees, you know.'

'Maybe the Communists had them all shot.' Tired of this dazzling repartee, Alexander returned to the Fat Slags.

Gary looked around him, already chronically under-impressed, at the clutches of hacks swapping hard-luck stories at the tables. Then his eyes stopped at a serving hatch. A young man in the clothes of a kitchen worker was staring at him, rapt. His cropped dirty blond hair, hollow cheeks and crazy eyes gave him the look of a smacked-out saint. Gary gave him a bit of retaliatory eyeballing, then moved on lest the wacko took it as an invitation. He turned to Alexander, started to ask him about Maria, stopped, looked around again and then decided to risk it. 'Listen, do you know a – '

His question ended in a shrill scream of pain. Beside him stood the wacko; running down his front, bound for his groin, was a jug of scalding hot coffee. He jumped to his feet and pranced uncontrollably with panic. 'Jesus Christos! What are you trying to do, neuter me?' The prancing had already cooled the coffee somewhat.

'Sir, I beg you! Forgive my carelessness! Please!' Looking more upset than his victim, the wacko grabbed Gary by the good arm and attempted to tug him hatch-wards. 'Come with me, I beg! Let me make amends! I clean!' As if to demonstrate his sincerity, he pulled out a filthy handkerchief and began defacing Gary's second best Reporter suit.

'No!' Gary wrenched his arm away and used it to knock the nutter flying. 'Leave it, will you?'

'But I can – '

'Keep it!' He left the canteen at a trot. 'What a bloody country!'

Alexander, watching him go, chuckled appreciatively. This was more like the English humour he'd heard about. This was more like *Viz*.

He'd been walking all afternoon, still at some pace, and it was all a blur; from his flat on Malá Strana where he'd gone to change into something marginally more comfortable than a skin-tight, sopping suit stinking of coffee and Czech nose effluent, through its whirling Baroque kaleidoscope of green domes and orange paving through the wooden arch to Wallenstein Gardens, a maze of paths and fountains named after Prague's most famous megalomaniac. He ought to have tried getting a job at the BBC – they'd soon have cut him down to size.

Past the grotesquery, with its aviary and peacocks (stupid strutting buggers) and along the path of sculptures by Adrian de Vries, he turned right down Letenská and passed the granite facade of the Finance Ministry, home of the good Thatcherite Václav Klaus. The Ministry was an extension of buildings which had belonged first to the Barefooted Carmelites and then to the Order of the English Virgins – he couldn't help thinking that the Divine M would get a good laugh out of that.

He passed through Malá Strana Square and past the Schönborn Palace to the Beseda, a Renaissance building which served as the unlikely haven of Prague's disappearing hippies. He stopped to gape at the Church of St Nicholas and was deterred from deciding to pray for a hot scoop by its gross grandeur. The last chapel on the left was called the Chapel of the Dead, where presumably the BBC sent his stories for a decent burial.

It was dusk when he turned right at the plague column – one of Prague's many homages to the saints who called off the Bohemian epidemic of 1715 – and left into Nerudova. It was less a street than a vertiginous chasm lined with Baroque and Renaissance façades, and yet again Gary was struck by the city's fantastic, grandiose resemblance to a colossal game of Dungeons and Dragons – or to one of those strange, totally impractical Medieval chess sets which were so intricately and ornately carved that you totally forgot what the pieces were meant to be and ended up with grandmaster ego on your face. It was without doubt the most beautiful city on earth; it was also completely impossible to operate smoothly in. It appeared to have been constructed solely for the purposes of dazzlement and disorientation.

Nerudova, for some reason, had more house signs than any other street in Prague – multi-coloured beasts, birds and surreally random objects which sometimes went back six hundred years. They had started as a peasant attempt to ape the stern disciplines of heraldry, but somehow – as they did in this city – things had grown a little wild and proud home-owners, desperate to keep up with the Jans in their bid for an original sign, resorted to biological freaks and zoological monstrosities. There was still a Stag With Two Heads – but not, Gary noted, a Beast With Two Backs. In 1770 the city fathers had called a halt to this collective craziness and introduced the revolutionary concept of house numbers; still, Gary couldn't help wondering what *his* little house in Nerudova might have been called. Hack With Two Faces or Rat With Nine Lives? And what about Maria? – how about Slag With Two Boyfriends? Thinking about her, he shivered and sighed.

Shaking himself out of his Electric Blue study and

attempting to lose himself in the role of tourist once more, he counted a Red Eagle – a scarey Rococo stucco; the Three Little Fiddles – ostensibly because three generations of violin-makers had lived there, though legend had it that satanic fiddlers gathered there at full moon (Gary wondered if they could help him fiddle his expenses) – now a wine bar. There was a Golden Goblet and a Golden Key and a Golden Horseshoe – but strangely enough, considering the decadent devil-may-care air of the city, no Golden Showers.

Thinking of dirty sex made him think of Maria again, surprise, surprise; it was dark now, and he was entering embassy country, which reinforced his thoughts. He wasn't in love, but he had a definite touch of erotomania. God, she was good. When would he see her again?

Up to the beautiful Romanian Embassy, past the not so beautiful Italian Embassy; surely some sort of joke? Past the blue-rinsed Bretfeld Palace apartments – even more than Rome, it was a city of palaces, pleasure and otherwise. If Romania was like 'Italians in hell' as one wag had said, Prague was like Rome in Disneyland.

The street suddenly narrowed and he walked in

hushed darkness. He made out a façade of the Holy Trinity, glorious – and huddled at its base, like some nasty post-modernist architectural trick, four skinheads passing a bottle of what looked like Chianti Mac around. All four wore huge Union Jack T-shirts, emblazoned with the words MADE IN BRITAIN.

'Welcome to dear old Blighty,' he muttered, shoving his hands deeper into his trenchcoat pockets and trying to look Western and tough. Too bloody Western and not tough enough, it seemed; a moment later there was the verminous sound of eight running feet, an inexpert blow to the back of his hard little head, a stumble to the ground, a roll-over. Four pairs of hands tugged at his overcoat, trying to get a bit of him. At last he knew what it felt like to be a pop star.

Then a voice yelled something threatening in Czech; a final kick – one to grow on – and they were off, no doubt to sample the recherché delights of Prague through a sophisticated mood-altering combo of Chianti Mac and cough mixture. Hell, he'd been young once himself. He groaned and clutched his groin, more in self-assertion than pain.

A man was kneeling beside him. He wore a camel-hair coat; he was fortysomething, and tall, blond, thin and Slavic. Not handsome but, in the manner of Christopher Walken, attractive in an unhealthy alien way. Like a fool, Gary flinched when the man reached out to touch his shoulder, as if from evil. He was obviously in shock.

'*Jak je Vám? Jste OK?*' the stranger asked urgently.

'*Ano, Děkuji.*' Gary stood up shakily. He checked his inside pocket. '*Ale ukradli mi peněženku.*'

'*Pojdte.*' The man stood up and took his arm. Despite his thinness, he had a good grip and a natural authority. He was not your usual Czech, and suddenly Gary knew; *Communist.* It explained the authority, the dominance and the expensive coat. One of the old guard. '*Potřebujete skienku brandy. Tudy.*'

They walked to a nearby, nondescript hotel; Gary sat shaking at a corner table while the comrade in the coat got them in. He took a huge gulp, and spluttered, 'Christ on a bicycle!'

The stranger spluttered over his firewater, too. And then he said, in a beautiful American accent, probably the only beautiful American accent Gary had ever heard, modulated yet unpretentious, 'Hey, the Queen's English! I thought you were a native!'

'I thought *you* were.' Gary was delighted, but not shocked; Communist, American, some sort of bossman.

'Me? No, just a humble tourist.' He lit a cigarette and offered Gary one.

'Take one – *Petra*. Havel's brand – forty a day man. Now *that's* the guy you want as leader. Not some jogging jerk.' He laughed. 'You know the cigarette etiquette in this country?'

'Not really.'

'Be careful about asking for a light. And don't take a live one from a Czech – unless you want to fuck 'em.'

Or unless you have; in his mind, Gary saw Maria handing him one of her precious Camels in the bedroom at the Hotel Evropa. 'Get away.'

'No kidding.' The American drank. 'Was the money in your wallet English or Czech, if you'll pardon the intrusion?'

'Czech.'

'Then those thugs did you a favour, friend. You

can't give the stuff away.' He finished his drink, signalled for another. 'You on vacation?'

'No, I work here.' Chippily, Gary tackled his glass again. 'Since last week. I'm with the BBC.' The brandy did a quick tonsillectomy on him; he tried not to cry. 'You're a tourist, you said?'

'In a manner of speaking. Doesn't this great city make gawping geeks out of all of us?' He held out his big, reptilian hand, a convoluted contusion of big blue veins and aggressive bones. 'Officially, I'm with the Embassy. LaMonte Johnson.'

Gary felt, for once, utterly English as he extended his hand without missing a beat. As they touched, electric sparks pushed them back from each other.

'Hey!' LaMonte jumped exaggeratedly, making light of a loaded situation. God forbid two healthy Anglos should mistake each other for fags. 'Is that a generator in your pocket, or are you just pleased to meet me?'

'Gary First. What *was* that?'

'It's these damn carpets – they wouldn't blow their noses on them back in my 'burg. Mind you, I wouldn't blow my nose on my *'burg*.' LaMonte laughed. He seemed a happy sort of stiff. The

Happy American. Well, natch. He had the free-hold on Maria Vachss, probably the most beautiful animal, vegetable or mineral in the world. Cowbag. 'So – you like it here?'

'It seems fine. More than fine – it's beautiful.' Gary told himself that, in many parts of the world, men walked on burning embers, and raised his glass again. 'But it's a mystery. And its skinheads leave something to be desired.'

'Ah, that element is next to negligible here.' Johnson gestured expansively. Or was it expensively? 'Unlike in my own fair city of Washington DC. Here, they mug you for money; there, they kill you for kicks.'

'But how long do you think it will take the Czechs to learn how to do that?'

'It's not necessarily inevitable; the East doesn't *have* to follow the West full tilt over the edge of civilisation, like a lemming on PCP.' Johnson's body suddenly changed; lost its lounge-lizard loucheness and strained forward, like a teenage Maoist at a Fifties Colombia University bull-session all-nighter, arguing for Red China to enter the UN. 'There *is* a third way, though you wouldn't know it from the Western press. I have great expectations of the Czechs – they're good people, and they're warm people; real genuine and uncomplicated. Not raving psychos like us.'

He leaned close to Gary; suddenly his passion was tainted by the temptation of male bonding. *That* was the first sin, Gary flashed suddenly; not Eve eating the apple, but the serpent saying – *hissing* – 'Oi! Adam! Ditch the bitch and we'll hang out – shoot the breeze on knowledge and all that jazz.' Male bonding made morons out of maestros.

Sure enough, Johnson delivered, 'And the girls are something else. Not just beautiful – they've got personality. Really know how to please a guy. *And* they enjoy doing it. That's the clincher. It's feminism's lost continent, Eastern Europe.' LaMonte leaned in even closer, if that was possible; one centimetre more and he'd get Gary pregnant. 'Seen one you like yet?'

Gary enjoyed the moment. Secrets; no wonder people became spies. 'Saving myself for someone special, aren't I?'

'Got a picture?'

Gary leaned back, nursing the drink which only moments ago had tried to kill him. He stared into space and saw Maria, tied to the bed, smiling at him in the candlelight. He smiled slightly, and looked LaMonte Johnson in the eye. (In the eye – what sort of cliché was that? As though the man in the mews was a Cyclops?) 'Only in my mind.'

Unbidden, Maria in different mode pushed her prostrate self out of the frame and snapped, 'Don't *drool*, gringo.' He blinked.

'A mystery girl, eh?' LaMonte looked worldly. Stupid fuck, he figured it was someone else's woman. Smart guy – he was absolutely right. ''Nuff said. And you say you find this place a mystery. Why's that?'

'I don't know – just being new here, I suppose. But it's more than that. Of course when you're new in any city you don't know what's going on. But in a place like this, where everything's changing all the time – I feel like I'll never get a grip on it. And then there are the other satellite boys, in Hungary and Yugoslavia and such, not to mention our man in Moscow. There's only so much Eastern Europe the radio can stand, and so we're all in there jostling for our fifteen minutes of fame and airtime every week. It's just really hard to pull away from the pack.'

LaMonte looked at him for a moment. Then

spoke. 'I could help you, if you want.'

Gary looked at him, surprised and slightly suspicious. 'Why? In a manner of speaking?'

LaMonte shrugged. 'Just call me the Good Samaritan – why not finish what I started? Besides, I hear a hundred stories in this town that I can't use; part of being a good diplomat is not being seen to spread gossip. And the US correspondents I've had the misfortune to meet here are prim little bastards who think they're being regular party animals if they risk a second glass of Perrier. I'm damned if I'm going to advance *their* careers.' He reached for Gary's empty glass and stood up. 'Another?'

Gary considered for a moment and then held it up with a radiant smile. 'Thanks. For everything.'

$\mathbf{I}$f anuses – ani? – could sing, Gary First's would have, now, after fifteen solid, succulent minutes of close attention from Maria Vachss. It sat there glowing smugly behind him as he crouched on all fours.

Maria lay on her back beneath him, her head raised against his groin, fellating him brilliantly. He felt like giving her three cheers; before he could organise it, he started to come.

At the critical moment, Maria jerked him out of

her mouth and aimed him at her eyes. He'd never seen *that* one before.

'You'll go blind,' he said as he licked her clean.

'Ah, but think how beautiful my last sight would have been!'

He laughed, kissed her and sat up to light the regulation cigarettes. As he handed her hers he said, perhaps too casually, 'Oh. Before I forget. I met your boyfriend last week.'

'He's not my "boyfriend".' She took her cigarette and rolled away from him, hugging a pillow.

'What is he, then? Your intended. Your green card. Your passage to fame, fortune and freedom.'

'He's my fiancé. Just say fiancé.'

'Sorry. We in the West find that word a bit naff. But I'll have a go.' He cleared his throat fatuously. '*Fiancé*. There. Does that make it allright?'

'It makes it respectable. It makes it legal. Which is the best I can hope for right now.' She rolled back and looked up at him. 'Where did you meet him? Embassy bash?'

'I wish! No – I was knocked down and robbed by a posse of your blood volk in Šporkova, as it happens. He saw them off. Very civil of him. Especially as I'm shafting his putative wife.'

She sat up swiftly and grabbed him by the shoulder, whirling him around to face her. '*What*? Why didn't you *tell* me?'

He was puzzled. 'Why should I?'

She turned away from him, a nasty smile on her face. 'No reason. Why should a john tell a whore anything?'

He grabbed her this time. 'What? Are you off on that one already?'

'What do you mean?' She shot him a poison look and wriggled.

He let go of her and scrambled off the bed, looking around for his clothes. ' "You never talk to me!" "We don't communicate!" Christ, Maria!' He pulled on his trousers, hopping foolishly.

'Don't blaspheme,' she said automatically.

He cooled down. 'There's more than one way of blaspheming, gel.' Fully dressed, he put his hands on his hips and glared at her. 'And you've just indulged in a fair bit of it yourself.'

'What do you mean?' She rubbed her thin arms resentfully.

He grabbed his raincoat. 'Exhibit A.' She looked at it dubiously. He shook his head impatiently. 'No, not this. *This*. We've been seeing each other twice a week, for two weeks – it's been great, but it's hardly a meeting of minds, is it?' Like what you had with Nikki and Miranda, a nasty little voice taunted him. 'And now, out of the wide blue yonder between your ears, you're coming on like a wife. What *is* it with women?'

'It's called being *human*!' She screamed it, jumping off the bed in the customised, haute couture variation on the birthday suit she wore so well. 'And yes, I know, it's a *terrible* flaw in our natures, that we care about people! It would be *wonderful* if we were like your side of the species, wouldn't it? If we could all treat sex like using a *spitoon*! Or a *toilet*! How very convenient that would make life for you!'

'That's it! I've had it with you, Maria!' In a rage, he grabbed his new wallet – Czech, horrible, made of unborn Communist or something vile – and threw a wad of *koruna* on the bed. 'There you go! Buy a pretty dress for yourself, darling! And an ankle bracelet, if there's any change. Cheers! Gotta go!' He did, slamming the door loud enough, if not to wake the dead, then at least to wake the night porter.

Maria stared murderously at the money for a moment. It occurred to her that she would not have believed that anyone could actually hate the sight of money. She picked it up, scrunching it in her hand.

A smile came first to her eyes, and then to her lips. She unclawed her hand and stared at the money thoughtfully.

He walked into the canteen, fresh from another binning from upstairs, set on drowning his sorrows in the house goulash. It was disgusting, but more alcoholic than a double Stoly on the rocks.

There appeared to be bubbles of laughter bouncing around as he took his tray and collected his liquid lunch. The nutter was gaping at him from the sanctuary of his hatch, as per. Gary glared at him darkly. If he tried any tricks with boiling fluid again, the only hatch he was going to be looking out from in the near future was the booby hatch.

The laughter and now some whispering built as he went to his table. He ignored it. In the unlikely event that he had stains on his trousers, the only cool thing to do was to act as if nothing was happening. To take the bait was death and dishonour. He got stuck into his stodge, stolidly. Alexander came in, collected his lunch and slid into the seat beside Gary. He took out the same copy of *Viz*; obviously he'd been instructed to learn it by heart. He propped it against the sauce bottles and smiled sideways.

'OK, Gary?'

'Yeah. I think so.'

Alexander started to fork food into his grin. Some of it fell out.

Gary looked at him, his insouciance evaporating. 'What's so funny?'

'Didn't you see your special delivery?'

'What delivery?'

'It's at the front desk. You can't miss it.' He looked around. 'And I don't think anyone did.'

'I'm in a work tunnel, aren't I? Trying to get just one story on air. I got in before the post this morning.'

'Then I think you'd better go and take delivery.' Food flew everywhere; he'd never read *that* copy of *Viz* again, that much was certain. 'Before one of the secretaries steals it!' Alexander cracked up helplessly.

Gary got up, overturning his chair. He was gone so fast that the kissing noises from the assembled hacks barely registered.

He scooted into the lift, and went down three floors to the entrance hallway. Everything was as usual, the two young uniformed security guards were behind the desk. The only thing different was that they appeared to be admiring a diaphanous scarlet dress, wrapped in cellophane, hanging on a wire hanger from a nail above the journalists' pigeonholes.

They looked across when they heard the lift doors open, registered Gary and doubled up. Too late, they attempted to exercise a little self-control as he strode to the desk.

'I believe that you gentleman have been kind enough to mind something for me?'

It was the foreign formality that did it; they howled, clutching each other like schoolgirls. One of them recovered in moments; the other collapsed face down on to the desk.

'Yes, Mr First.' The savvy guard gestured wildly at the dress. It was slashed to thigh and navel, frilled and ruched – the party dress of a hooker from Hell. The guard took it down and held it out to Gary, his face contorted by his superhuman effort to suppress his laughter. 'Shall I wrap it for you?'

'No, I'll frigging wear it, won't I?' Gary snatched it from the man as though they'd been tussling over it at Harrods' sale; the guard collapsed on top of his compadre.

Gary made it to the lift, and made sure the doors were stuck tight. He held up the dress and found a note pinned to the neckline, which was somewhere at crotch level.

'TI AMORO – YOU LEFT THIS. LOVE AND XXX, MARIO.'

He was out of the lift and back at the desk. 'Is Maria Vachss in the building?'

The strongest guard nodded, waving at the signing-in book, still too weak to speak. Gary grabbed it and cased it.

Up two floors, he walked along the corridor peering through the small glass panels in each door. There she was, the bitch; typing, her hair pulled back, wearing a huge pair of headphones. She looked up as he slammed the thick door behind him, then back down.

'Can't stop!' she shouted. 'I'm in a work tunnel!'

'See?' he yelled back. 'You even talk like me, you bitch! You talk like me, you screw like me, you think like me. You even hate like me! Though even *I* wouldn't have thought of this!' He threw the dress at her; it landed on the typewriter, forcing her to stop. 'Out there like that! With everyone sniggering behind my back. And in my face.'

She threw the dress on to the floor and ripped off the headphones. Sitting down, she actually stamped her foot. 'Just one face? Why not both?' She typed, blindly. 'Anyway, the dress was your idea. "Buy a pretty dress" – remember?' She stopped pretending to type, rested her chin on her hand and looked at him coolly. '*You* threw the money on the bed, no? Or did I extract it from your pocket, like a proper English whore?'

'I remember.'

'Funny.' She started to type again, controlled this time. 'I know that's meant to make *me* a whore. But I thought it made *you* one. That's why I bought you that dress. Didn't you like it? The most whorish dress I could find – for the biggest whore I know.' She looked up. A diamond ran down her cheek. 'OK?'

Looking at her, it suddenly happened. Or maybe it had happened already – that first day in the Slavia, or that first night in the Evropa, and now suddenly he just knew about it. Whatever, he was in love. He laughed, stupidly, like a fool. It was so fucking simple. Like falling off a log. Though he'd never fallen off a log, being a city boy. Like taking a crap. Like scoring your first goal. Like being born. It was the simplest, most mysterious thing in the world. Why had he been so stupid, to spend so much of his life being smart? He was in love. This was where his life really started.

He laughed again, his new village idiot laugh. Global village idiot. Maria's face misted as she looked at him curiously. He blinked, scrunched his eyes up, as though trying to evict a bit of grit. Then his vision sharpened, and he saw her slightly open her mouth. For the first time, he didn't think of shoving his dick into it. She had a chipped front tooth, the right hand one. How had he been so stupid as not to notice? He grinned smugly, as though he had unlocked the secrets of the universe.

'You broke your tooth.' He smirked, like an

American orthodontist about to become a rich man.

'What?' She looked embarrassed; her pale skin actually took on a pink tinge. A girl who blushed. The only girl in the world who rimmed *and* blushed. How could he *not* love her? 'Yeah, I fell off my bike when I was nine. So what?'

'What colour was it?' He smirked again.

'Red.' She said it as slowly as one can say a word of one syllable. She had realised that something was new. 'Why?'

He relaxed, and smiled. It felt like the first time he had ever really relaxed enough to smile genuinely in his life. He thought of all the lying smiles; to get girls, to get liked, to get work. It was shocking. The words lay in front of him, like a box of chocolates composed solely of his favourite centres. He approached them luxuriously, glad now he was a virgin. He really *had* saved himself after all. 'Because I love you.'

There was the sound of muffled clapping from behind him; he turned, and through a wall of glass saw three bearded young men, the technicians who had been feeding Maria the radio stations she had been transcribing so skilfully. They gave him assorted thumbs-up and hi signs; he looked back at her, still smirking. It was brilliant.

She smiled up at him, half happy, half scared. 'Congratulations, Gary. We've just gone public.'

'Get naked.'

'Say *wha*?' He looked down at himself. 'What's this? Top hat and tails?'

'You know what I mean.' She threw a pillow at him. 'You read American books. Tell me about yourself. Properly.'

'Tell you the *truth*? Fuck me, that's a hard one.' He snuggled down and crossed his hands behind his head, grinning at her. 'You're cute, you know that? You're not really as ugly as people say. Go on, you go first.'

'OK.' Naked, she crossed her legs and looked serious. 'My name is Maria Vachss. I'm twenty-five years old. My parents work in factories. I share a bedroom with two small sisters, whom I love and want to murder. I believe I have some Jewish blood – my parents deny it. Anyway, for as long as I can remember, I've felt different. Like I was passing for normal, all my life. I'm blonde, I have brown eyes. This is an unusual pigmentation combination, thought to be the female ideal in medieval England. I'm beautiful. I've got bad breath – no, don't deny it.'

'Darling, I wasn't going to!' He spread his hands, wide-eyed.

'Pig.' She laughed, and became serious again. 'I'm scared of dentists. Doctors. Men in white coats everywhere. I'm superstitious, I'm intelligent, but probably unoriginal. I'm narcissistic, but I know somewhere inside that I could never really make it in the West alone. I'm scared. I'm ambitious. I'm so glad I'm alive. I'm engaged to a rich American who will take me away from all this. I'm Czech, I wish I wasn't. I'm in love with Gary First, I wish I wasn't. And I'm just so fucking happy for the first time in my life.' She put her face in her hands; laughing, crying, the whole cream cake.

He looked at her; she didn't spook him any more, but he felt more respect for her, and more desirous of winning her approval. Oddly, her vulnerability had made her more authoritative; she was so strong that she could show her weakness. He decided to play it straight. 'Gary First, twenty-five. English and fucking proud of it. Fantastic fuck, scoopmeister extraordinaire. On the fast track to Top-of-the-Heapsville. In love with this girl, Maria Vachss. She's none too bright, and if the truth be told she's a frigid old boot with about as much sex appeal as a two-day-old teabag. But what the hell? At least she's no trouble.'

She took her hands away and smiled at him. Her eye make-up was smudged, giving her an unbearably slaggy look. Blonde hair clung to her swollen red lips. How could a woman be so fucking beautiful and not explode? 'Again. With feeling.'

He pulled his eyes away from her, looked at the white ceiling and let all the mundane pain come flooding back. 'I'm English, I'm twenty-five years old. I was born in North London. All my life I've known I was a phoney. I've always pretended. At first I pretended my parents loved me. They didn't. My mother miscarried three times. By the time I made it, she was worn out. Naturally I was a disappointment. But they were brave. They worked like dogs – they worked in factories, too – to support a growing mortgage and a thriving series of insurance policies. I never wanted for anything, except a bloody book, or a word of encouragement. I realise it's a lot to ask from life. They were working-class. They did their best. I wish they were dead.' He covered his eyes, grinding the heels of his hands into them. 'I'm so disappointed with myself. I can't begin to tell you the dreams I had when I was twelve. Before I become good old Gaz. I wanted so much to be a writer. But I can't do it. I can't make those fucking words dance. I'll always be a hack.' He wiped the tears away, and with the spirit of the young and beautiful beloved brightened quickly. 'But to be fair, on the other hand, I love this life. And young English male novelists look like crap. And I came here.' He looked at her, blinking. '*And* I met you.'

She was crying; she draped her face over his, and their tears mingled – a very good year, in interesting times – and she licked them away. 'You are so beautiful. Do you know that?'

'Yes.' His sorrow had become hers; unburdened, he got up and went to the window, for the third time that night. 'Are you sure?'

She nodded, yes.

121

He looked back at her, then again to the window. 'But I *feel* someone's watching me. Not just here. At work. In the building.'

'Not the techies.' Maria dried her face on the sheets, feeling Eastern and over-emotional. She had noticed it before; they recovered so quickly, Westerners. From words, from wounds, from wars. 'They're nice guys. And they have no reason to make mischief. They don't know LaMonte; they've only seen him once or twice, when he's picked me up from the building. They don't especially like him.' She lit a cigarette. 'In fact, now I come to think of it, no-one does.'

'Not even you.'

'Very funny.' She reached for the ashtray.

'I liked him, though. He actually offered to put a few stories my way. Did I tell you that?'

'No,' she said, very sharp.

He couldn't believe it. Not again. 'What's wrong?'

'You're not going to *let* him help you, are you?'

'Why not?' He meant it.

She smoked, silent. 'Aren't you taking advantage of him enough already?' she said after a while.

He was amazed – shocked, actually. His awkwardness made him rude. 'What a touching display of loyalty.' He looked at her. He wanted to stare her out. 'You use him. Why shouldn't I?'

'Go to hell.'

'Sorry, no can do. Got to stay here for two years. I thought that's what this was all about. No? Yes?'

She said nothing.

'Look. I even use your charming little yes/no gimmick at the end of each line.' She didn't bite. 'Yes? No? Go on. If it's not sporting to use the poor bastard as a career contact, why's it pukka to use him as a passport?'

She wheeled on him. 'You really don't know, do you? You really haven't heard a word I've said. I'm not marrying LaMonte because I *want* to – I'm marrying him because I *have* to. There are a lot of men in the West who want to marry Eastern girls, you know – should I go to one of the bureaux that's suddenly sprung up, where they give you introductions to a bunch of boobies who've paid for the pleasure? A lot of educated women are driven to it – doctors, teachers, lawyers. They could probably pay their own way in the West, but they're not given work permits. Until they marry.'

'I've seen the adverts, in magazines. It used to be Filipinas.'

'Well, now the inflatable sex doll comes in white, too. But it's just like it is for the Filipinas – they end up married to slobs who want sex six times a day and don't even give them any spending loot. A lot of them run away and have to take menial jobs.' She laughed bitterly. 'Some of them even come back *here*, poor bitches.'

'Go on.' Was this a story he saw before him?

' "Go on" – "I'm here" ', she mimicked. 'You're a real hack, aren't you? Don't think I haven't got your number. I'm just another human interest story to you, no?'

'Miss Vachss,' he said solemnly, taking one of her hands in both of his, 'I can assure you that this is all in the strictest confidence. Just you, me and twenty million World Service listeners.'

'Pig.' She thumped him. 'It's not funny. Some girls do get to the West by themselves; they end up on drugs, as prostitutes, you name it. But if you marry the right guy, you're in clover. I know a girl who married a dentist, in Aspen, Colorado? Last month she went up in a ski-lift with Sylvester

Stallone.'

'Get away!'

'Yes, you think it's funny.' She was defiant. 'But only because you've never gone without those things.'

'Oh, you're spot-on there, gel. I grew up in an Aspen ski-lift, I did.' He brushed back her hair and looked into her face. 'You're a clever woman, Maria – a lot cleverer than me. So how come you play so dumb on this one? The myth of the Blessed West. There's poor people where I come from, you know. There's poor people and homeless people and people with no hope at all.'

She stuck out her chin, combatively. 'Then let them come here. And give those of us with some guts left the chance to go for it.'

He got up and went to the window again. There was no-one watching him, of course there wasn't. Then why did he feel as though he was under 24-hour surveillance by MI5? He turned back to her.

'But even if your techie mates did sing, or even if he saw us together with his own eyes – it wouldn't matter now, would it? Not now we're in love. Because he's going to find out anyway.' He walked across and stood in front of her. 'Isn't he?'

She smoked in silence, not looking at him.

'Maria?'

She looked at him, hard. 'If I break my engagement, will you take me to London?'

'You know I can't.'

'We'd have to stay here?'

He nodded.

'How long?'

'You know how long. Two years. Tell a lie – one year, eleven months and one week.'

'Two years … ' She gazed off into thin air, stubbing out her cigarette. Then she jolted, like someone waking from a bad dream, and swung her legs to the floor. 'I can't.'

'Why not? Afraid you'll miss the ski-lift?'

'No!' She was dressing, faster than he'd ever seen anyone dress before. 'Afraid I'll *die* in this place, that's why! Afraid I'll wake up one morning, and I'll be losing my beauty, and I'll be losing my eyesight, and I *still* haven't seen anything better than myself. I hate this country! Hate it!'

She was fully dressed now, and she snatched up her handbag and began to prowl the confines of the room as though looking for things to put in it, bumping into the bed, the walls, the closets, and not noticing.

'I can't stand to think about the promises they made – and the garbage they've given us. I hate Havel. Redesigning the uniforms for his toy soldiers, hanging out with the Rolling Stones – disgusting, ugly, washed-up old pigs – while his people rot. I can't stand that the streets are full of the filth he let out of jail, trying to be a big man. Amnesty! You can't be a Communist in this country now – but you can be a rapist, a murderer, a child molester and still walk free. And be guaranteed a job!' She stopped prowling and turned on him ferociously. 'Did you hear about that pig, at the hospital, that Havel had let out of jail? First day on the job, he raped a sick seven-month-old baby! Then he fell asleep, drunk, on top of her! He killed her. *Havel* killed her. Thank you, Mr President! On your motorbike! In your uniform! While the children of Czechoslovakia lie raped and dying!'

She screamed the last word in his face, as though he was the good President Havel himself. Then she swallowed, and took a step back, still staring at him.

'And Wenceslas Square. Look at it! Under the

Communists, three hundred thousand people were there day and night, keeping vigil to bring down the Government. Not one person hurt, and it was a revolution! Now you take your life in your hands when you go there – last year, a gang of two hundred beat up *two* Canadian tourists. Canadians! Oh, brave Czech people! The police have to clean the swastikas off the Wenceslas statue every week. But really, why bother? We have a president who *apologises* to the Germans for the Krauts who were thrown out of Sudetenland after the War! After they had *raped* our country! A president who shakes hands with Waldheim!' She ran her hands over her yellow hair distractedly. 'Look at me – maybe I'm not a Jew. But I feel like one. I feel *disgusted* by the way our own president doesn't seem to remember what the Germans *did* to us! We should be taking our anger out on *them*, if we have to – *they* started it, the war that made the map the way it was. But instead we're licking their boots, and a lot else, hoping they'll leave their marks on us. Deutschmarks this time. And all our anger is wasted on innocent tourists, stabbed in broad daylight for their spending money. Killed! And you thought I was being hysterical when you got robbed!'

She fell down on the bed and put her face in her hands. He sat down behind her and stroked her back.

'Murder doubled since the Communists went,' she went on mercilessly. 'Rape almost doubled. About a third of all police sacked because they might – just might – have been Communist. All the jobs disappearing through privatisation. It will take decades, they are saying, to build this country up to where it was when the Communists were in. And by then it will be too late.' She turned to him. 'I'm not a Communist. I hated that grey life. But I hate this more. All the danger and sadness of the West, and none of its solace. Don't I *deserve* a consolation prize?' She grabbed him by the shoulders and shook him violently. He let her. At that moment, he would have let her inject him with the HIV virus if it would make her feel better. 'Don't I deserve *anything*? – just for being born in the wrong place?' She gave him an almighty shove and collapsed on her front, sobbing.

Then she looked up at him, and her wet face was a moist mask of determination. It was impossible to feel sorry for her now; to understand her was all she asked. 'Gary, I love you. I'd kill for you. But I won't die for you. And for me, staying here another two years would be the same as dying. Dying by degrees.'

8

Prague's Schönborn Palace was started in 1643 and finished in 1656, and remodelled by Santini at the beginning of the eighteenth century. During the nineteenth century it crumbled into disrepair and was rented out as apartments to commoners. For a few months in 1917, one of its tenants was Franz Kafka.

The Schönborn Palace brought a smile even to Kafka's face; he wrote to his fiancée that his was 'the most marvellous apartment I could dream of

... I have electric light though no bathroom, no tub, but I can do without that.' Famous last words; five months later he went down with tuberculosis. Now it was the American Embassy, and Shirley Temple reigned supreme.

'It's a metaphor, isn't it?' Gary suggested snootily to Maria after reading all about this in his invaluable *Cadogan City Guide* to Prague. 'About Europe, being screwed by America?'

She had looked at him coolly, seeing right through his jealousy and pretension. 'No,' she said after a moment. 'And it's not a metaphor for me being screwed by LaMonte either, if that's what you're insinuating oh-so-subtly. It's just a nice story. Can't you ever leave anything at that?'

'No.'

Now he saw Ambassador Temple Black across the biggest and most beautiful room of the Schönborn Palace. She really was a beautiful older broad; the most beautiful broad in the room apart from ...

There she was, wearing a red dress, drinking champagne, laughing. Not his red dress, though; if his was made for a hooker from Hell, this one had been created for the queen of Madame

Claud's. Disgustingly demure, high in the neck and low at the knee, it hugged her so hard and so strategically that in the US of A she could have slapped a sexual harrassment suit on it.

She saw him, and ducked back into the crowd a place she was never meant to be. Fair enough. A little drunk already, he sipped the bad champagne and cased the scores of well-dressed, well-heeled and probably well-hung expats who buzzed around a buffet that would not have disgraced a Rothschild wedding. Prague was the Paris of the East, and attracted the successful in search of sexy sorrow, that much was clear.

He saw an African ambassador, tall, dark and handsome, flaunting his tribal robes like a Rolex. A giggle of white women, mostly English, surrounded him, mesmerised. He was talking about democracy. His wife, who wore her robes like the Chanel suits she usually dressed in, looked on with bored disdain. Looking at the women through her eyes, Gary could tell that she was braving her boredom by betting with herself which one of the white women her husband was sleeping with. He was now talking about the importance of keeping the African race pure. The beautiful black woman consulted *her* Rolex Oyster and yawned, quite openly. Gary saw them as young, passionate freedom fighters, newly in love, and felt sad.

Then he laughed. An Arab was stealing some silverware. A short swarthy man in short shirtsleeves and no tie, obviously an Israeli, tapped him on the shoulder and shook his head. The Arab replaced the spoons and looked at the Israeli with respect and resignation. Gary had a flash of feeling he often had about the Israelis, while not being of the blood royal; that they were your team, and you supported them right or wrong.

A tall Chinaman and a short European, both beautifully suited, were talking not far from him. Their young wives, who wore near identical black cheongsams, stood by them, bored senseless. The European girl, a delicate blonde, looked at the Chinese girl and touched her slender nose almost imperceptibly; then she inclined her head towards a staircase. The China girl nodded and grinned. They whispered in unison to their husbands, who didn't appear to notice, and scurried away hand in hand, like bad children escaping a stuffy grown-up gathering. Which of course it was.

A snooty Frenchman inspected the buffet,

gingerly selected a canapé, took a bite and made a face. He looked around, and placed the savaged savoury back on top of the pile.

A waiter dropped a plate. A Greek diplomat beamed, and followed suit. Gary laughed out loud, enjoying himself. Then stopped as he saw LaMonte, his hand raised in greeting, leading Maria towards him. He gulped champagne. It's *showtime*, he thought grimly.

'Hi, soldier!' Johnson clapped him on the back, making him choke. 'How's the war wound?'

'Fine, thanks.' He grinned weakly. 'Never felt better.' Until you hit me in the kidneys, you stupid American fuck. And brought your tootsie over here to torment me with. Bitchily, he thought about her bad breath. Pathetic. It didn't help. God, he loved her.

'Stout fellow.' Johnson was wearing some sort of dark red suit. It should have been a mistake, but wasn't; his lanky, blond, albino thoroughbred looks and Maria in red by his side somehow made it work. Gary realised suddenly, and unpleasantly, how physically similar they were; tall, blond and thin, with strange slanting Slavic faces. Of course, he was old enough to be her ... father?

135

'Oh-*kay*.' LaMonte grinned from one to the other. 'First things first. Gary, may I introduce you to my fiancée, Miss Maria Vachss. And Maria, my dear, this is Mr Gary First, Esq – young shaver I told you about, I believe. Works for the mighty BBC. And Gary, Miss Vachss is the most beautiful girl in Czechoslovakia. Which means *the world*.'

'Hello.' She held out her hand. God, she was cool.

'Mutual, I'm sure.' They shook. Their palms made a rude noise as they parted.

'Manners!' LaMonte cackled. Then mugged. 'But what am I saying? You kids are already acquainted!'

The lovers locked eyes. At that moment, they were ready; to deny, to defy, to deck Johnson and run away. It passed, as he said, 'You *must*. What with Maria and her work for the BBC.'

Gary smiled cheesily. 'It's a big building, Mr Johnson. And I'm sure I'd remember Miss Vachss, if I'd ever met her. Even for a nanosecond.'

'You bet your buns you would.' LaMonte laughed smugly. 'OK – it's boozing time. Be right back.' He twinkled, horribly. 'Don't you kids get up to anything!' And was gone.

Gary watched his back disappear, then whispered to her, 'What's all that about, then?'

She was embarrassed, which was unusual. 'He's always like that. With every man we meet. Shows me off like a cross between a proud father and a pimp. It doesn't mean anything. Don't worry about it.'

'Worry, me?' He smirked, enjoying her discomfort. 'And I see we're wearing our lovely white slingbacks again! The dress has got to be American, the tights are bound to be French – but those lovely shoes are a little piece of Czechoslovakia wherever they go, aren't they? What is it with you two? Three, rather.'

'Walk a mile in them, Gary, and maybe then you'll start to understand.' She glinted at him, motor revving.

'How about it, then?' He was drunk, and coasting on their intimacy. Did Johnson notice her shoes, how they clashed with the rest of her game plan? Never. The cubic old crumblie just

137

presumed that those were the shoes a sexy Slav would wear. He didn't see how anachronistic they were, how they jarred with her refined beauty. 'In the khazi for a quick one? There's already a pair of designer dykes in there doing blow. That's where the real party is.'

She smiled slightly, uneasy. 'You're crazy.'

'Crazy for *you*.' He sipped his champagne and grinned. 'This is weird – seeing you with your clothes on.'

'Mutual, I'm sure.' She looked around the room nervously. 'Listen, why don't I introduce you to a nice girl?'

'Because I've already *got* a nice girl.' He stared at her murderously, then grabbed her by the arm, digging his nails in and meaning to. 'Come with me.' He waved off his sanity and sobriety; it was a relief.

'Stop that!' she hissed. 'You're hurting me!'

'You're hurting *me*, you evil fuck!' he hissed back.

'You said it! We agreed! ' She wasn't wearing it. 'If we fall in love, we finish! Well, we did! And we are!'

'You're declaring unilaterally, just like that? Don't I get a say?'

'You had your say!' she barked angrily. She looked around, then hissed, 'You had your say! And you said you wouldn't take me to England! Now let go of me and walk through that door like a good boy, or I'll scream. I hear the ambassador packs a rather enthusiastic brace of bodyguards; you're going to look pretty funny with your nuts stuffed up your nostrils.'

'Don't worry, you conniving little bitch!' he snarled. (Barking, snarling, fucking like rabbits; they were a regular little menagerie, let alone a *ménage à trois*.) 'I'm not sticking around here to watch *you* offering blow jobs to all and sundry in exchange for a green card!'

'Pig! The only green card I'd get from you would be from a VD clinic!'

Alexander passed by with a glass of champagne and a Russian redhead, obviously bent on discussing Soviet domination of Czechoslovakia. He twinkled at them, but there was warning in his voice. 'Speak up, children – our good President can't *quite* hear you, all the way over there in his palace.'

'Listen to that!' Gary hissed at her. 'Every hack in this town knows what's going on between us!'

'Then every hack in this town has got it wrong, as usual! Because there is nothing going on between us – nothing at all! And if you dare to tell my fiancé that there is, I will deny it! And Katya will deny it, and the technicians, and everyone! Because we may not have much here, but we stick together! You may be able to buy our bodies, but never our hearts and souls. Or our minds!' She was as drunk as he was, he realised in dismay. What an excruciatingly naff speech. Where had she found that one, *Thoughts of Chairman Havel?*

He laughed, enjoying his feeling of superiority for once. 'Buy your minds? You couldn't give 'em away, sweetheart! You dumb bunch of peasants make the Arabs look like frigging Renaissance men!'

She slapped his face, hard, like a mean drunk in a bad B-movie. He gasped. Everyone was looking. And a brace of bodyguards was bearing down on him, hip holsters bulging. Well, *they* weren't pleased to see him, that much was certain.

Confident in her cavalry, Maria gave it a final twist. 'Don't you *dare* talk about my people like that! Get out, whoever you are!'

'Watch me!' He tried to push his face close to

hers to give it extra force, but they had him. Light as a feather he was gliding across the polished floor, smooth as Katarina Witt but not to a perfect triple 10. Instead, to a pair of wooden doors thrown wide and the merciless mauling of a gravel drive.

The doors slammed; they sounded almost human in their smug triumphalism, and it sounded almost personal. He stood up and glared at them. 'And the same to you! With doorknobs on!'

Drunk and stunned, he glared at them for a moment longer before walking down the drive towards the street. Pitch black, as per. Obviously the Government believed that street lighting was some sort of collective Communist evil.

Without warning a bony hand shot out, like a skeleton's mitt in a ghost train. But it didn't just trail over his face; it clamped over his mouth, and a knife was pressed against his cheek. His goons – LaMonte's goons. Gary said his prayers, or at least the Desiderata. It was the only religious thing he could think of at such short notice. He'd just got to the part about being a child of the universe when he was dragged behind a clump of foliage and pushed face first to the ground. His hands were held behind his back, painfully.

Talk your way out of it, he told himself. It was a bit difficult, with a mouthful of dirt. 'Please … I don't … '

The goon whispered in his ear, a Czech accent, familiar. 'Listen! I must talk to you!'

He decide to use his killer wit. 'Couldn't you have called first, and let me consult my Filofax?' He swallowed a mouthful of earth, and retched it up again.

'I could not wait, I say! This is a matter of life and death!'

Gary turned his head slightly. 'You're not a journalist, by any chance?'

'No! – *you* are! BBC, right? You are BBC man?'

'What do you want me to say? I'm easy, honest.' This wasn't a goon, was it? Hope dawned; was he going to get out of this with his manhood intact, or what?

'Aha – humour under pressure!' His attacker sounded approving. 'The acid test! Yes – you are BBC man,' he acknowledged graciously. 'I watch you, in canteen. And you go in and out of Evropa Hotel, many times, I am right?'

His heart did a triple back somersault. A goon.
A watcher at windows. 'OK. I'm BBC man. What
you going to do, kidnap me? Cut off my broad-
casts? I warn you – I'm new at the job. New and
useless. I'm not valuable. You won't get much in
the way of ransom.'

'Ransom?' The goon tutted irritably, like a
shopper given the wrong change. 'What is this?'

'Moolah. Bish-bosh. Dosh. *Money*.'

'Why you talk so?' The goon was well teed off.
'That's not English! BBC men not talk that way!'

'They do when they're wetting themselves.' He
wasn't, but he would if the script called for it, and
if it was tastefully done. 'Could we go somewhere
more comfortable and chat, do you think? There's
a nice warm police station down the road.' He
tried a sarcastic snigger, double bluff, and got
another mouthful.

'British humour again, I see.' The goon
sounded cheerful, not chippy. 'OK, my friend. We
make deal. You promise on honour of BBC you
don't run away; I promise I don't hurt you.
Gentleman's agreement, right?'

'Certainly.' Promise 'em anything, then run. 'I
can see you're a man of your word.'

His hands were freed; the knife went back from whence it came. The pressure left his back and Gary sat up, shaking. He got to his feet carefully, rubbed his cheek and looked daggers at his assailant, in the dark in more ways than one. 'OK. And if this *isn't* a matter of life and death, it soon will be. Because you'll be a dead man, pulling that for no reason.'

'I wish it *was* my death in the balance.' The assailant's voice came out of the darkness, melodramatic and pious yet with real yearning. 'But it is not.' He fumbled in his pocket and the beam of a tiny, tacky torch came on. Another fumble, and it was shining on to the extravagant handwriting of a grubby letter. The man's face was still obscured. 'Read.'

Gary looked at it, then shook his head. 'It's Czech.'

'You don't read Czech?' The man sounded shocked. 'But you are – '

'Yeah, I know.' Gary bristled chippily. 'BBC man. I *can* read Czech, right? But not when it's this colloquial. And hand-written. Especially in hand-writing that a drunken spider appears to have dragged its wet feet all over before passing out.'

'It's from my sister, Ava.' His voice grew mushy. 'My little sister. She goes to America – ' he pronounced it like Rita Moreno in *West Side Story* – 'to work as a receptionist in a big hotel. So far so good – letter every two weeks, happy as all get out. But I don't know. Parents *want* to believe the best – but something not right. I tell them so eventually and they look at each other – "He's off," you know? Then last week, this – ' He pointed to a line of the letter and mumbled something Czech to himself, as if trying to translate. 'This line here. How I explain? In English, I suppose nearest would be "Tell that to the Marines" – you see? Is way of saying "Don't believe a word of it!" If a foreigner who read Czech were to see it, they wouldn't get it. But that's the point. So why she have to use such a device? Because someone is reading her letters. And this is normal? In the land of the free?'

Gary had been listening to this monologue with some scepticism; the guy was a nutter, that much was obvious. Nutter, the word jogged his memory's elbow, sending boiling coffee cascading over his mind's eye, and he took his lighter from his pocket, flicking it into life. It was Twinkletoes, the clumsy canteen worker, his cropped hair – of a colour usually described as 'dirty blonde' but perhaps more accurately in this case 'filthy blonde' (a bit like Maria Vachss, heh heh) – hollowed cheeks and crazy eyes once more evoking a smacked-out saint. Only this time, a saint in the last stages of loss of faith, pitiably distressed and utterly convinced. A look of resignation came on to Gary's face; he could *feel* it, squatting there like a self-righteous toad. He knew, without doubt, that once again his heart was proving not half as hard as he'd hoped. Some armour for this *amour propre*, no more *amour*, he thought idly, and then was shocked. He *must* be in love – spouting frigging haikus like Miranda gone mad. Whatever happened to his shopping lists of the heart?

'What's your name?' he asked the loon wearily, like a righteous but jaded copper who'd seen too much too young.

The nutter beamed; it transformed him, giving him a saint-in-ecstatic-trance look. He still looked loopy, but happy-loopy. He obviously knew a soft Western touch when he saw one, like all these bouncing Czechs and sly Slovaks. 'Tomas, Tomas Kavan. And my sister is Ava Kavan.'

dealer uses monster as servant – and to guard his beautiful daughter. Monster, as they will, falls in love with her and goes on rampage of terror, with broken heart. Smashes shops. Terrifies citizens. Finally he bursts through glass doors and chases girl to top of a tall tower. She snatches Star of David from his neck and he turns back into statue, falls from tower and shatters to smithereens on sidewalk below.' In the light of his lighter's flame, Gary saw Tomas sit back on his heels with a rather self-satisfied, that's-life expression on his mush.

'Women, eh?' tut-tutted Gary, feeling it was expected of him.

'Oy, is not her fault. Is not Golem's fault, either. Is insensitive people around them ruining their love, putting obstacles in their way ... '

'So you're telling me that this babe would have happily laid this clay giant with the filthy temper if society hadn't frowned on such unions?'

'Yes.' Tomas wasn't being moved on this one. 'She was a *spirituelle* girl. Not caring for worldly things. Seeing only the true beauty at the heart of the monster ... ' His voice was dreamy. Obviously a bit of identification going on here. 'There are such women. I know ... '

'Well, it's a good job she didn't get it together with him, isn't it?'

'Why?'

'The guy obviously had feet of clay. And in hot weather, his cock could snap off.'

Tomas looked at him, offended. 'Already you mock!'

'Pardon me for breathing. Listen, I've got to go soon. You've got two minutes to tell me what you and this Golem geezer have in common – apart from the fact that you obviously went to the same charm school.'

'Two years ago, I have trouble.' Suddenly he was serious again. No, not serious; make that suicidal. Gary wondered whether his shoes had laces, and began to work on a subtle strategy for getting them away from him. 'Break up with girl I love – Nadia. Very *spirituelle* – father a priest. Evil old shit. Hates me. And then, it's also my own fault – wandering eye. Worse, wandering hands! But when she won't see me, I realise at last how much I love her. And I go crazy. I dress up as Golem, in rags and clay, and go around city at night, scaring people. Nothing sexual, you understand – I am true to my love. Just to frighten – men, women. But never children.' He looked at Gary for approval.

Despite himself, Gary laughed encouragingly. 'There's a good Golem.'

'You don't laugh at me!' Tomas objected without conviction. He gathered his thoughts and continued. 'So, after a while, I am captured. Probably through kind offices of Nadia's pig of a father after I visit her home dressed as Golem one night and smash window because she won't see me. Most likely locked in bedroom by vile-smelling old goat. So police come, and I am put in jail. I cannot tell you my mortification – three to a cell, sharing a bucket for toilet and absolutely no clay whatsoever.' He looked at Gary, his mouth trembling.

'Shocking.' Gary did his best not to titter.

'Ah!' Tomas held up one finger and looked sly. 'But then comes Havel – and the amnesty! And I am out! But things are not as before; now people don't trust. And not just Nadia and the goat this time, but my own family, and my friends. So definitely not police, you see? Only my sister, Ava, loves me as before. For the rest, every time I open my mouth is sniggering – "Yes, Tomas the Golem, and what is your crazy idea now?" I can't even get the job I've been studying for – and I am first-class graduate in law.' He sighed theatrically. 'So now I work in your canteen, which of course you know.'

'I'll say.' Gary remembered. 'Well, law's loss has been catering's gain.' A thought struck him, not unpleasantly. 'And you've been following me, right? Watching me, at the Evropa and all! I knew I was being watched – I thought it was my girlfriend's – boss,' he finished unconvincingly.

'Girlfriend's boss?' teased Tomas. 'Why would he watch you? Is she sleeping on the job? Or perhaps sleeping with the – '

'Fancies me, doesn't he?' said Gary tersely. 'Get on with it then, Golem – this is your story, not mine.'

'That *is* the story.' Tomas sounded quite offended. 'I know you are BBC man, and I think you look … special. I see you don't sit with men in groups and laugh about women; I see you sitting alone a lot, thinking hard, and I feel I can trust you. End of story.'

'But can I trust *you*? A convicted nutter who prances around Prague pretending to be a monster?'

'That is over, I tell you!' Tomas struck the ground with the heel of his hand. 'Temporary insanity! I am completely myself once more.' He clutched at Gary. ' And I need your help.'

'But I'm just a journalist ... ' Really, all things told, did he need this?

'No!' proclaimed Tomas triumphantly. 'No, you are *BBC* journalist! You don't know what BBC *means*, especially in this part of the world. It kept us going all through the dark times. From lowest to highest person; when the coup kidnapped Gorbachev in '91, remember what it was he said? "Luckily I find radio in house and can tune to BBC. Then I feel better, to *really* know what's going on!" '

Gary laughed, amused by the young nutter's enthusiasm. He was flattered, but not entirely convinced. 'I don't know ... listen, I'll be honest with you. I've got to think of myself here, OK? My job, I mean. I don't want to waste time following up crazy – ' Tomas winced – 'false leads. Even more, I don't want to make a prat of myself –

155

come across like a screaming mimi.'

'Excuse. What is mimi?'

'Nutter. *Sorry*, OK? But look at it – kidnapped sisters. Non-existent husbands and addresses. It'll be the white slave trade next. What I mean to say is – it's hardly the sober, World Service political analysis I was sent here to do, is it? If you're as familiar with the BBC as you say, you'll know that that particular branch of it doesn't go a whole bundle on human interest stories.'

'But suppose it is the *truth*!' Tomas looked around wildly, as if for proof or perhaps a gallon of scalding liquid with which to attempt a little gentle persuasion on his prisoner. He lucked out, and brought his equally burning gaze back to Gary's face. 'Weren't you sent here to tell the *truth*, above all things? Isn't that what the BBC *means*?'

Gary stared him down coolly, then shook his head. 'You poor deluded bastard. OK. Give me the letter.'

Tomas smiled beatifically, pressing the letter into Gary's hand while the other hand clasped his shoulder painfully, digging in with passionately bony fingers. 'You will not regret this!' he swore.

'Running fool's errands for a bloke who thinks he was made on a potter's wheel? I doubt it.' Gary got to his feet and began to brush himself down fastidiously. 'You win. I'll check it out, and give you a nod in the nosebag if I get a whiff of anything. I'll leave a note under my plate; time, place, all that. That do you?'

Tomas jumped up, embracing him horribly. 'Yes! Yes, it will be done! Goodbye, my friend!' Then he stopped, holding Gary at arm's length. 'You would never betray me, would you?'

Gary threw back his shoulders – not too big, but nice and square – and straightened his Georgina von Etzdorf tie. It was partly grand gesture, but partly real pride in what he sensed was a growing ability to handle himself – and others. 'What, me? Me, BBC man? Do me a favour.' He thought of something. 'Your sister – got a picture?'

'A minute.' Tomas fumbled in his overcoat and handed him a dog-eared, smeary colour snapshot of a girl with long blonde hair smiling back over her shoulder. He looked at it, and saw Maria's insouciant stare of sexual sedition; then the mist cleared from his eyes, and Ava Kavan was once more just another healthy young heifer with pop eyes and rather rabbity teeth. Nevertheless, it shook him. So he looked at Tomas seriously, and said, 'Trust me – I'm a journalist.'

9

He placed the call to London, and sat in the flat on Malá Strana – some tongue-twister – biting his nails, and enjoying it too. It was a habit he had always associated with neurotic people – or girls. Worst of all, neurotic girls. Well, maybe he was becoming one. That was just too bad.

The phone was ringing in London – eight, nine times. In a shabby, welcoming flat in St James, with *Gardeners' Question Time* on the radio and a Marks & Spencer Spotted Dick steaming on the stove. England! Suddenly he missed it so bad he could taste it, taste the stray currants catching in his teeth. He cursed the ambition that had brought him here, and lost him love. Still, better not knock it. Ambition was all he had left now.

Eleven, twelve. In the old days, when he'd been a kid on fast-forward, he only let a phone ring three times before binning it. And now he was just about to put it down after a dozen bells when –

'Hello?'

It was an angel's voice. Male, middle-aged and marbled with bloodshot veins of pure alcohol, but an angel's voice nonetheless.

'Hello, Edmond?' he gasped excitedly, a boy calling for his first hot date.

'Who's that?' Edmond asked gruffly. Drunk as a skunk, as per this year.

'It's Gary – Gary First. I took over from you, remember?'

There was a silence as the windmills of Edmond's mind ground slowly into action while trying to avoid the nasty little hangover imps with hammers who were doing their damnedest to tilt viciously at them. 'In Bangkok?' he said finally.

'No!' (You pathetic old lush.) 'In Prague. Four

weeks ago.' He tried harder, risking flirtation. Thank providence that the old bender was 650 miles away. 'I had some sort of bloom, apparently. But I bet you say that to all the boys.'

'But of course, *mon brave.*' The old pervy sounded a lot more interested now. 'Hang about, I think I remember you. Good-looking boy, dark brown hair. Pushy.'

'Self-motivation, they call it now, sir. It's the sex appeal of the Nineties.'

'Give me a well-toned bum any time.' Edmond cracked up at his joke. Gary hoped he choked on his Spotted Dick. The old sod was making him feel like a phone-sex bimbo. In his mind's eye Maria appeared, mocking him obscenely with an anthropologically interesting two-handed gesture she certainly hadn't learned out of *The Art of the Deal.*

'Listen, Edmond ... Mr Crichton ... sir,' he stumbled on. 'I need your help. Some pointers on a delicate subject. Is this time of day convenient for you? Or should I call back?' When you've emerged from your drunken, masturbatory stupor, you washed-up old berk. He kept his voice honey-dripping. 'You tell me when.'

Gary could almost hear the rheumy old bones creak as Edmond Crichton drew himself up to his full height with no mean helping of drunken dignity.

'If by "convenient" you mean am I sober? – no, if it's any of your business. But I don't need to be sober to think straight.' Gary heard him swig smugly. '*Au contraire*, Pierre. Go on.'

Given the go ahead, stage-fright struck. 'It's hard ... I feel stupid ... ' He bit his nails again. Talk about a movable feast. What was wrong with him? Gary First, never last. For the first time in his life, he was actually thinking before acting. And it was a major drag.

Edmond, sensing weakness, took over and bullied him amiably. 'Well, lad, what d'you want to do? Write me a postcard? Thought you didn't want to be penpals – '

Gary gaped. 'You – '

'Yes, I remember every word you said. Surprised? Flattered? Don't be. I've got the much-boasted, rarely hosted photographic memory. Fed it on a bottle of Bombay gin basic – with wine and brandy supplements, that's very important – every day since I was twenty-two. Pack of lies about brain cells; alcohol *preserves* them. Can't teach it, just got to have it.' He drank again. 'But one thing you should have learned by now is to get to the point, preferably yesterday. Are you a journalist, or are you keeping a journal? Spit it out, lad.'

Gary swallowed a thumbnail, spluttered, then spilled, all in a rush. 'I met this guy … Tomas – I can't tell you his full name, not on the phone … '

'The Communists have gone, Gary.' The voice was as gentle as Edmond's ever had been. It occurred to Gary that he wasn't really hitting his mark, if the ageing lush he had deposed could feel sorry for him.

'Yeah, but the Government's still there.' Thank goodness for cynicism, the last refuge and resting place of the thwarted, embarrassed idealist who'd been smart enough – if only it *was* smart enough! – to drown his dreams at birth 'Well, this Tomas – he's convinced his sister's been kidnapped. Some sort of – I don't know what to call it but white slave trade, from East to West. From Czechoslovakia to America. It's happened before, apparently. The girls think they're going feet first into some cushy marriage, through some cowboy bureau, and then they end up on the street, strung out on junk and what have you.'

163

'Well, *drugs*,' hiccuped Edmond profoundly. '*Messy*.'

'Right. Well, this guy's sister, she was meant to be married to some solid citizen in Chicago – '

'There *are* no solid citizens in Chicago – '

' – with some part-time talky-smiley gig as a receptionist in a big hotel. Dead kosher. But now it turns out the home and husband never existed. And the hotel never heard of her.'

'Curiouser and curiouser. Where do you fit in?'

'He wants me to help him trace her. And the people who shipped her out.' He stopped, and heard silence from the other side. It made him have a pathetic attack. 'Hardly *From Our Own Correspondent* stuff, is it? More *News of the Screws*.' More silence. A triple, with chaser. 'Do you think I'd be mad to help him?'

Edmond spoke slowly, and suddenly seemed extremely sober. 'No. Not at all. No-one ever went broke over-estimating the value of a human interest story. Especially one with lashings of sex, drugs and slavery.' He topped himself up. 'He's reliable, your source?'

Gary closed his eyes, held his nose and jumped recklessly into Edmond's gin, trying not to hit the rocks. 'OK. This is the tricky bit. He's – he's a nutter. Did time for dressing up as some sort of clay monster – '

' – the Golem? – '

' – and creeping up on people in the dead of night. There was this big amnesty – '

' – Havel – '

' – and he got let out, but natch, no-one listens to him now. Except me. And God knows why I did. I've seen for myself how unstable he is. Damn near mugged me and dragged me behind a bush to tell me his tale of woe. Dutted up the shmutter something rotten, and then expects me to help him. Just because I'm what he calls "BBC man." '

There was mischief in Edmond's voice when he spoke; all at once Gary could hear him as a young man, sending over bottles of vintage Krug to wide-eyed and long legless young sailors somebody who knew Francis Bacon had brought up to the Colony Room as a lark. 'But you *are* going to help him, aren't you?'

He started to object, then gave it up as a bad job. 'I suppose so,' he shrugged, not wanting in the least to appear heroic.

'Then he was right, wasn't he?' Edmond gurgled, though whether he was laughing or choking on his own drunken vomit was unclear. 'How mad can he be, showing judgement so sound? Maybe his instincts are good on other things, too.'

Somewhere in St James a doorbell rang, drunkenly and with prolonged indecency.

'Ah, the fleet's in. 'Bye, dear boy.'

'Edmond – '

'And take care.' The phone went dead.

As Maria Vachss had already told Gary First in no uncertain terms in a bedroom in the Hotel Evropa, one of Václav Havel's first acts as president had been to sign an amnesty releasing some 200,000 criminals, not a few of them rapists and murderers, from jail. It was a typically macho, dramatic and thoughtless act – Maria, in moments of despair, said that it shouldn't have been called the Velvet Revolution but the Dralon Revolution, seeing as Havel was such a phoney baloney.

This, combined with the fact that the demoralised police force – the VB – had been virtually forced into hiding in the months following the 1989 coup, had conspired to make Prague as chancy as any other European capital after dark. With typical melodrama, many residents now referred to it as the New York City of Central Europe.

The VB had been disliked for its enthusiastic support of the Communist Government, its strict, almost surreal enforcement of the jay-walking laws and its alleged stupidity – there was to wit the old Prague joke that the city's police patrolled in threes because there had to be one to write the arrest warrant, one to read it, and the third to keep an eye on these two, probably subversive, intellectuals. Four years later there was still a widespread suspicion of the boys in green – but it was fading fast as crime rose and the VB abandoned their old excesses. Increasingly, the cars which bore the legends VB and POLICIE brought with them relief rather than fear.

Pickpocketing was rife, the thieves working inevitably in pairs – probably the only communal effort that took place in Prague these days, unless you counted bought sex – wherever tourists gathered to gawp, and especially on the Charles Bridge. But the ugliest scenes of unbridled violence took place after dark each night in Wenceslas Square, the cradle of the coup, and on the green in front of Prague's main station, known as Sherwood Forest. The pimps and punters of these places, plus Perlova Street, made them a grim gauntlet for any woman without a male protector – pimp or otherwise. And as for anyone the 'wrong' side of beige, nowhere was plain sailing; Gary had heard the word 'nigger' more in four weeks in Prague than he had in a previous four weeks spent in Atlanta, Georgia. The thirty thousand Vietnamese resident in the country and the few hundred thousand gypsies who had survived the Nazis lived under a ceaseless campaign of hate.

It was into this worsening state of affairs that Gary now stepped, gathering all his courage with a slender – a bit too bloody slender; whoever said you could never be too rich or too thin had obviously never been faced with selling a toughened police force a story that couldn't *be* any richer or any thinner – file of Czech press cuttings on the mysterious disappearances of young women (precious few; as though Czech society didn't really believe that *any* move to the West, manacled or not, could be that bad) and Western press cuttings on the springing of drug-addicted Eastern bloc women from sleazy brothels. Not to mention his ace in the hole, of course; the letter and photograph so thoughtfully provided by that most reliable of witnesses – or should that be 'witlesses' – Mr Golem Schmolem Esq, of Serving and Booby Hatch renown – and took this incontrovertible little bundle of happiness along to Prague's central police station at the humourously – named Konviktska in the Old Town. But not, of course, before making a date with the clay-footed one himself.

The phone rang.

'Right on time, comrade.'

'I found the note, under your plate! This is serious? We go to see police tomorrow?'

'It wasn't easy. When it comes to the West, your lot are like the three thick monkeys. See no evil, hear no evil, speak no evil – the guy I spoke to at the desk practically refused to admit the existence of one missing Czech paper-clip stolen by a Westerner. Let alone a string of young women for immoral purposes. But he listened, eventually. The BBC still counts for something, you above all people will be pleased to hear.'

'You want me to come at one o'clock to his office, note say. We are to go separately?'

'We could go together, but I'd like to get there a bit beforehand – show him my file, such as it is, prepare the ground if I can. You just come in and be your eloquent old self.'

'Yes.' He sounded down; what was up?

'What's wrong? Isn't this what you wanted?'

'The police … they know of me. What will he say when he sees it is me?'

'He'll see a man who cares desperately about his sister. Who's vanished into thin air. That's what he'll see. He'll see a file as thick as my dick – well, not quite – of similar cases. And he'll see a hack who's going to shame him into getting on to the trail of these scumbags toot sweet unless he wants a prime-time piece on how his country cares less about the live export of its female population than it does about its cattle blasted all over the free world. Not good news when your economy depends on Western handouts, I think you'll agree?'

'Yeees ... '

'Right!' He paused, then spoke. 'Come on – we *are* BBC men, no?'

Tomas burst into laughter, but it seemed tinged with tears. 'Gary, I will never thank you!' It probably wasn't meant as ungraciously as it came out.

'Easy peasy. Just turn up on time and be yourself, right? Tomorrow?'

'Tomorrow.'

Then everybody hung up.

Officer Hus had that look of disgusted decency which is common to police officers of a certain age the world over. Only he had literally a head start; he was the spitting image of the world's greatest living film actor Gene Hackman, who invariably played disgusted decency personified.

Now he directed the bolshy, flickering beacon of his disgusted decency across his big, battered desk at Gary First. The file lay between them, not declaring an interest.

'OK.' Hus sighed. 'You have a point. But these girls, in these clippings here, are found. Men punished. Cases closed. What more can *I* do?'

Gary leaned across the desk, while still keeping a respectful distance. This was a man you didn't bandy cheap stylistic devices with. He spoke urgently, trying to call up the patriotic knee-jerk defence of the countrywomen's honour that lurks inside most men, especially unreconstructed types. 'These girls were found when they were *junkies*. When they'd been taking on twelve men a night for ten months. There isn't a cure for that sort of injury – most of them are still junkies, still whores. So why not try prevention?'

Hus shook his head. 'Mr First. The relatives of these girls are not coming forward in their hundreds. They *want* to believe that they have daughters in America with swimming pools and barbecues. It is, as you say, a status symbol – the next best thing to having it yourself. Unless these girls are actually found and videotaped lying unconscious on a bare mattress with a hypodermic syringe sticking out of every orifice, it's very hard to convince them it is so. And every girl who claims she has a Western fiancé – I am supposed to run a check on each one? Do you *know* what our workload is, since the glorious revolution came? We don't need that sort of trouble. We want other sorts of trouble, we can take our pick.'

Gary decided that it was time for his best shot; strong-arming by any other name. 'Sir, I'm a journalist – I have to tell what I see. Do you really want the tender-hearted people of the Western world, on whose good will your country depends right now, to see you as some sort of Philippines on the Danube? It's hardly very *European*, is it? It hardly brings you into the family of free white nations.'

Hus narrowed his eyes even further, if that was possible. He considered, then spoke. 'OK, Mr First. We play it your way for a moment.' He pulled the photograph of Ava across to him and looked at it. 'So here we have a real missing girl. And a relative willing to think the worst, for once.' He smiled wearily. 'And do you know who this oh-so-reliable witness is?'

Panic poleaxed him. Hus knew. 'His name is Tomas Kavan,' Gary stuttered. 'He works – '

'Also called the Golem.' Hus produced a second file and placed it, like a killer card, on top of Gary's. 'Also prances the streets of Prague at night frightening women and children.' He tapped the file. 'You know this?'

'It wasn't women and children,' said Gary, sounding surly, hating himself for it and powerless to stop. 'And it was a long time ago. He's better now. He was let out under the amnesty.'

Hus snorted. 'Please. That is hardly a recommendation. Every other madman and murderer I see was let out under the amnesty. Now it's only the lawful citizens of Prague who are serving a life sentence. Why couldn't our beloved President have kept his fantasies for the stage?'

'Sort of street-crime theatre,' Gary quipped pathetically. Maybe it lost something in translation, but Hus shot him an evil look. 'Please,' he pleaded. 'Just wait till you talk to him. Then judge him.'

Hus looked at Gary, and seemed about to dismiss him. Then he stopped and shrugged. 'All right. You win.' He took a packet of full-strength Sparta cigarettes from his top drawer and offered one to Gary, who accepted. 'You like this country, Mr First?'

Gary beamed. 'Thanks.' He took a light, feeling that Hus was offering even more. 'Not *like* it. But – '

Hus laughed, making the interruption friendly. 'You're right – like is the wrong word. They say – '

Suddenly there was a jagged rainbow of screams from the outer office. The door swung open.

There, swathed in bandages, dropping stray clay on to the carpet, was Tomas, the Golem, in all his gory glory.

Gary walked across the Charles Bridge, oblivious to the trippers and tourists. In his hand he gripped the file he had laid so lovingly at the feet of Officer Hus less than an hour earlier, so tight that it appeared he was attempting to strangle it.

Beside him ran Tomas, weeping, his bandages flapping. The famous bridge had seen thousands of fairs, fiestas and even coronations, but no sight could have amused its crossers the way the costume of Tomas the Golem appeared to.

'Please, Gary!' Tomas pleaded, tears streaming down his bandaged face. 'Let me explain!'

'I can't hear you!' Gary kept walking, not turning his head. 'You've been dead for four hundred years!'

'Gary! I beg of you!'

His distress was so extreme that Gary, despite himself, stopped and looked at him. The creature spread its hands in despair.

'I just couldn't stop myself!'

'Tell that to the judge next time you're hauled up for impersonating a dead guy!' Gary thrust the file at him. 'And show him this!' He started walking once more.

'Gary, it was my girl!' The Golem was scampering beside him now. 'The one I loved and went crazy over in the first place, remember?' He waited for an answer and didn't get one, so went on. 'She got *married*!'

'Who to?' Gary stopped and faced Tomas one more time. 'An American, by any chance? What is this, another disappearing act? Like your alleged sister? Do you have a photograph of this woman which I can take back to my friend the police chief, who by now trusts me and my judgements implicitly? Or maybe you've just got a bee in your bandage about women leaving you. Maybe you need a shrink, not a hack.' He started walking.

This time Tomas made no attempt to follow him; he just stood there, like a child, weeping as Gary went on alone. 'Gary! Please!' he wailed.

'Keep it!' called Gary over his shoulder, moving

smartish. 'Go and scare some children! That's all you're fit for!'

'Gary! I'm sorry!' By now the wail no longer seemed human, but totally in keeping with the costume of the tormented spirit.

Gary stopped for one heartbeat, and he looked back for a minute with his voice quiet and quite, quite hopeless. 'I know.'

Then he walked off the bridge, and out of his life.

10

It must be a wrong number. It must be, because the phone was being picked up! Saturday night in sexy greedy London, and the phone was being picked up! So of course, it couldn't be –

'Marco Bondini. In the flesh, and twice as fresh. This is not a recorded message. But if you're a boring twat, or want to borrow money without interest, I'll hang up anyway and then where will you be? Go for it.'

Gary took a breath. 'Marco? You make the Speaking Clock sound like the Samaritans. It's me. Gary!'

'Homeboy.' Marco sounded slightly let down, which meant you were a real mate and was a compliment in a way. He was forever expecting the call which was going to make or break him. Friends could merely bore him. He heard Marco drop on to his tarty leather couch. 'How's it hanging?'

'Crack or career?'

'Whatever, whatever. Good times.'

'Career pretty bad, if you want the level. I can't get a handle on Factor X – what it is that's really happening here, beneath the skin. The Czechs and Slovaks have split, in theory, but there's no civil war … '

'Shame.' Marco's tone was amused, almost mocking.

Gary realised how whiney he had sounded and pulled himself up soonest. 'No. Of course not. It's great that they're sorting it out like adults. But – '

'But it makes your job a good bit harder, is that right?'

'In one. No news is good news. Which is no news.'

'Yeah, I thought you'd been a bit conspic in absentia from my World Service orgies.'

He heard Marco light a cigarette and thought longingly of the West, where everything was simple. 'I miss you,' Gary said thoughtlessly.

There was a silence. Then – 'FAAAG,' pronounced Marco, clearly and slowly and beautifully, as though performing an elocution exercise designed to stretch the lips and jaw to their fullest extent. His voice was merciless and very, very formal. 'Now listen, baby brother, and listen like good; I may slag off women something awful in public, but if – and I said IF – I want to bare my bollocks, I'll do it with them, right?'

'Right.'

'Right.' There was an awkward silence which Marco somehow contrived to let Gary know was entirely his fault. 'Listen, I know where you're at – I've read about this "men talking" crap too. But as far as I'm concerned, men talk about one thing – women. Not their feelings, not their emotions and certainly not their aching bollocks, job-wise. Got me loud and clear?'

'Got you.' Gary's face was red.

'Good.' Gary could hear Marco mentally

straighten his tie, getting ready to proceed to the next matter in hand. 'Because if you've quite finished spilling your guts, I've got a tip for you. Semtex.'

'Say wha?'

'Semtex. Plastic explosive. Brown, very pliable, like putty in your hands. A bit like that Persian bird I was knocking off July last. Two pounds of it with a detonator in a plastic lunchbox attached to the underside of a posh car with a magnet, and Irish eyes are smiling. Bob's your uncle – and John Paul's your pontiff.'

'It's not all Irish people who – ' Gary said automatically.

'I know, I know. Laughing boy. OK – IRA bastards' eyes are smiling. More accurate, I'll give you, but it kills the flippant fluency. As a writer, you ought to get your priorities in order. Anyway, Semtex is the world's numero uno plastic explosive – and it comes from none other than the glorious country you are now billeted in from here to eternity.'

'I know all that.' Gary tried hard not to sound impatient. Sound impatient with Marco and he'd pull the plug on you once and for all. 'But they've stopped exporting it now the Communists have gone. Havel came to ' (still 'came to', not 'went to', he noticed – a sure sign of a homesick heart) 'London in 1990 and made a big speech about it. Never again and all that.'

'All that old tat.' Marco snorted. 'True, true. But Havel's only – was only – the Government. Do you really think that the military will let go of their lovely little earner so easily – or even the men who run the economy? They've got to balance the books somehow. Give up Semtex without a struggle, just because their bosses are getting all touchy-feely with the West? Tell that to the Marines – if they haven't been blown up with Semtex yet.'

Gary's throat was dry. 'Go on,' he rasped.

'Thing was, I sussed things weren't going too well your side of the Danube and I guessed you might call for a bit of moral support and parasitism. So I took out my business acquaintance Andre – '

'Andre the arms dealer,' Gary twinkled.

' – I took out, as I was saying, my good friend Andre, a commodities broker of some repute, for a light supper at Christopher's. Asked him what the lay of the land was in Czechoslovakia – '

Her name's Vachss, Maria Vachss. And I love her ...

' – and he said the lay of the land was Navratilova. But only if you're a bird. Sorry!' Marco's apology for his lousy joke came touchingly fast, and Gary felt guilty that he had immediately thought of a variation on the same smutty theme.

'Go on,' he said again.

'Andre says this; think Semtex. Sell Semtex, buy Semtex, sniff out Semtex wherever and however you can. 'Cept it's odourless. That's the advantage to smuggling it in. The West has been working on this computer – called SNOOP – for airports, but it's far from being a sure thing.'

'Why?'

'This stuff is just so weird; no smell, no shape, no show on the X-ray. Some A-rab once took it on a plane disguised as an attaché case; just moulded into the shape of one, with a few zips stuck on. Carried it on his lap like a nipper all the way. Got caught at Customs when some sharpie stuck his fist through it, natch. But no-one on the plane noticed anything out of the ordinaire. Can you believe this stuff?'

'No. Which means it's a great story.'

'Right. So it's made in this town called Pardubice, at a plant called Semtín. About sixty miles east of Prague. They had ten thousand people there working round the clock to produce twenty thousand tonnes a year; equiv to a small atomic bomb. The factory's hidden behind a forest, Andre thought. Sounds a bit scenic to me.'

'And it's still going on? Business as usual?'

'Ah, of course they've got their shtick ready. Havel comes over and says, Whoops, the Commies supplied the international terrorist community with enough sexy Semtex to last them a cool hundred and fifty years – but it won't happen any more, honest! And they spend those long working weeks at the Semtín plant "researching ways to make Semtex more detectable" – they say. But why bother to make it more detectable if you're not even supplying it to the bad guys any more?

'In 1989 the Communists themselves swore they hadn't exported any of the stuff since 1982! Were they on the level, or what? Then how come there's enough Semtex at large in the world to blow up every commercial aeroplane in the West ten times over?' Marco snorted with a sort of appalled respect. 'Course they're still pushing it. It's their thing. It's damn near their only thing, apart from tennis players and poncey playwrights – and even they seem to have dried up a bit now. You sell what you have to sell to survive; Semtex, smack, crack. You don't stop to think about what it might do to other people – you can't. Survival is a spotlight – it shuts out all other vision.'

'Marco, your Double First is showing.' Gary said, very quietly and with the utmost respect.

'Bastard. That's the last time I blow the price of a light lobster supper on your cockamamie career. Got to go – slapper to saveloy. Remember; Semtex – seek and you shall find the story. Dig you later, masturbator.' There was a massive plastic explosion in Gary's left ear and the line went dead; it was still big in Marco's circle to gain extra power-play points by slamming the phone down before the sucker on the other end. Very Eighties.

Gary didn't care. Marco could slam down fifty phones a day on him and Gary would beg him to bang them even harder so long as he kept it coming. Trust an Eighties boy to go straight for the beef every time.

A feeling which seemed like part patriotism and

part homesickness swept over Gary. But it was easy to accept and assimilate, simply because it was so impossible to lose. It was a longing for a place which, unlike England, he could never go back to. It was a longing for the easy, sexy, greedy Eighties themselves.

To escape from his sickness, Gary read. He raided the BBC reference archives and steeped himself in Semtex.

It had been first sighted in Britain in 1972 when an Arab terrorist used it to murder an Israeli diplomat; since then it had been the slippery, sly first choice of both the IRA and the Middle Eastern homeboys. The Arabs and the IRA shared a particular interest in cowardly ways of killing people, and Libya made the IRA a present of five tonnes of Semtex some time in the Eighties.

Semtex is the filet mignon of explosives; it is twice as expensive as dynamite, but immeasurably more cost-effective. Two ounces of it can do the same damage as two hundred pounds of conventional explosives.

Brown and putty-like, it differs from other

plastic explosives in that it cannot be detected by either sniffer machines or sniffer dogs, and does not show up on the most sophisticated of airport X-rays. It is so malleable that it can be moulded into the linings of handbags; so stable that it can be held next to a naked flame without exploding. It keeps extremely well; in 1989 four bricks of Semtex weighing 22lbs each were found on the newly drained bed of a London waterworks. It was still usable.

In 1984, Semtex was used to bomb the Conservatives at the Grand Hotel in Brighton. In 1987 it hurled a coach three hundred yards along a road in County Tyrone, killing eight British soldiers. In 1988 it was used to bomb army barracks in London and Shropshire, and 150lbs were found with a list of prominent targets in a London flat. London begged Prague five times in 1988 alone to add some pungent impurities to the explosive, or to give it a chemical fingerprint which would make stray, murderous batches more detectable.

Also in 1988 a Pan Am flight exploded over Lockerbie in Scotland, killing two hundred and seventy-one people. This time, Prague offered to send explosive experts to help identify the cause of the tragedy. Of course, it was too late.

In March 1990, the new President Havel of Czechoslovakia announced on a visit to London that his country had sold, in all, around one thousand tonnes of Semtex to Libya. But of course, it wouldn't be that way any more! The death of Communism and all that jazz – jolly good chaps together!

If only it wasn't for the continuing discrepancy between the amount of Semtex exported by the official government agency OMNIPOL and the amount which left the plant in Semtin; around 360 tonnes at the last count. Still, Havel was a clubbable chap, and so was his successor now the bad guys were gone, and Czechoslovakia and Britain could easily connive to conceal such embarrassing statistics next time an innocent British soldier was blown to pieces in the IRA's psychotic scramble to give the waiting world just what it needed – yet another Catholic country. Such deaths, after all, were not the province of men of government; foreign relations were far more important than grieving relations.

Gary First rubbed his red eyes with his white

knuckles, hurting himself and meaning to, trying to banish tears, tiredness and guilt all in one go.

He had his story.

Everything was going to be OK.

11

'What are you thinking about?' The common currency – no, the loose change of the international exchange. Was there one woman on earth who didn't ask this question sooner or later? It seemed to him that Maria alone could make the cliché feel fresh.

They lay on the bed at the Hotel Evropa, shiny with sweat, like prime auditionees for a lousy Adrian Lyne film. All it needed was Ry Cooder on the soundtrack, the black Venetian blind and the motes of dust dancing in the sunlight – *9½ Inches*.

'Begins with S, ends with X,' Gary said lazily.

'I've got it!' She rolled over on her stomach and brushed back his hair from his brow. 'Semtex, right?'

'How did you know?' He gaped at her, a touch cretinous, and then rolled away in search of a cigarette to hide his gaucheness.

'What? ... I was joking.' She sounded very foreign, as she always did when confused. 'Why do you think ... ?'

'What's the joke?'

'Well, obviously ... ' She laughed, embarrassed. 'Naturally, I thought you were thinking about sex. Our sex. That we've just had. That's why it was a joke – that sex and Semtex begin and end with the same letters but obviously you weren't thinking about ... ' She shook her head as he offered her a cigarette; probably a Czech first. 'Why were you thinking about Semtex?' she asked slowly, looking at him.

'I'm fascinated by it.' He struck a match, lit up. 'It's going to be my big break. My big story. The discrepancy between the new promises and the same old sharp practice. There's this amazing statistic which practically proves that – '

'This is a joke, right?' She sat straight up in bed, her body following the arching arrow of her voice, the sheet falling away in awe, her beautiful breasts bare. She looked like a designer pirate ship's figurehead carved by Allen Jones and about to be photographed by Bob Carlos Clarke. 'You wouldn't be dumb enough to tell me this if you were … '

'Maria, Maria!' Panicking, his first response was, perversely, to try to calm her down. He grabbed her by the shoulders. 'You're losing me, angel! What's the problem? What did I say?'

'You know where I come from, don't you?' she blared at him. A blare, he decided, was a cross between a glare and a blame.

'What? … Prague… '

'No! Not bloody Prague! What a mindless, utterly lazy thing to assume!' She jumped out of bed and stamped a foot; they were long and amphibian, a little like plastic flipper feet. The vibrations did spectacular things to the rest of her. 'You don't even know where I come from, do you? That's bloody typical of our relationship!'

'Why? Where do you come from?' Was she a

Kraut or a Russian, and touchy about it? He racked his brains for things he might have said about either racial group. Or were they the same? Come to think of it, that was probably the worst thing you could say to either of them.

'I come from Pardubice, you fool! Pardubice!' She threw back her tangled blonde hair and sneered royally at him.

'Oh. My God.' He let go of her.

'Yes, my God!' She grabbed him now; her strength, which was generally impressive, seemed always to double itself when she was naked. 'Yes, imagine – I'm the girl from Pardubice! Probably as tall and lovely as the girl from Ipanema, if not as tan and young! But twice as useful when it comes to coping' (she meant copping, he registered with dazed adoration) 'a good story, no?' She began to scan the room for her ex-clothes; when she did this, which she did a lot in the spats they had after sex, he could easily picture her in a Communist uniform; her, and a searchlight. She *was* a searchlight.

'Maria!' He took a chance and caught her by the wrists. She turned her head away. Her blonde hair was so coated in sweat it looked black in parts. 'I swear I had no idea. Honest! Would I really have come out with that Semtex line if I'd known?'

'A bluff.' She turned her head to him but lowered her eyes, still frowning.

'Bluff, my muff!' he snorted.

She looked up, surprised, and laughed.

He did too, but with relief, eager to consolidate this apparent change of humour – however flimsy. He was home – or he would have been, with any other girl. But perhaps Maria was just too mobile – perhaps there *was* no home with her. Which was, surely, his dream situation.

'Maria. Listen. Mindless and lazy it may have been – that sounds like a pretty good working description of me – but I swear that I honestly assumed you were a Prague girl. To me, you *are* Prague. I never *dreamed* you were some Slovak peasant girl, on my life.'

'I'm not a Slovak, I'm a Czech,' she mumbled. 'Pardubice is in Eastern Bohemia; as you well know after your extensive research.'

He let that one go. 'Why don't you come and sit down and tell me all about it?' he murmured soothingly, leading her naked to the bed. She followed, but she was still sneering silkily.

'Look at you!' she mocked. 'Stark naked, ten minutes after sex, the sperm still seeping from your dick, and you're in search of your big story still!' But she kept following him.

'Who, me?' he mantraed, sitting her gently down on the bed like an invalid, or someone who had just had a bad shock. (Which she had; that her boyfriend was a heat-seeking hack from Hell.) His mind was going at a rate of knots. Keep calm – go slow – don't give her an excuse to bolt. 'Anything you want? Drink? Cigarette?'

'I could murder one of your heads on a plate and a half bottle of Roederer Cristal to wash it down with, as you're asking.'

He chuckled. 'That's my girl!' He sat down beside her, taking one of her hands in both of his. He was aiming for a sort of benevolent bedside manner approach. A bit like Dr Crippen. 'Now. Why don't you tell me all about where you come from, and all about your family, and then I'll tell you all about my interest in Semtex. Then we'll have it all above board and no nasty secrets and suspicion spoiling things.'

She looked at him dispassionately. 'God, but

you're bad at being caring, Gary. Keep on being a bastard. It suits you better.'

He chuckled urbanely. A demon seducer she wanted, a demon seducer she was going to get, the slant-eyed Slavic bitch. 'OK – level with me. Give me what I want ... and I'll give you what you want.' You berk, he cursed himself, you sound like a parody of some cretinous singing stud who ends up doing an Isadora when his medallion catches in the wheels of his Mas.

'A ticket to the West, you mean?' she spat, and he was shocked to see a tear trickle from her eye and land heavily on her knee. Bugger. He'd gone and blown it with that slimy shtick.

'Maria, Maria,' he said miserably. 'Listen – I really don't want to play games, or roles, or whatever. Let's just talk – as you and me. I'm after a Semtex story to take home to my masters; you come from the only place on earth where they make Semtex. Why don't we just pool our resources and see what we can do for each other? As friends. Sound good to you?'

Her head jerked round, her sweat-stringy hair whipping him in the face. 'What do I get out of this?'

'What? … well, what do you want?' He was surprised, and felt stupid for feeling so.

'Money. Cash.' Her voice was hard. 'So I have some money of my own when I marry LaMonte. So I don't have to be a complete whore.'

'OK. I'll try.' Did she have any idea of the World Service's budget? She'd make more – perish the thought! – from five minutes in a Mercedes with a merciful Kraut from across the border.

'Right.' She clenched her fists, looking ahead of her at the wall. 'Pardubice is about sixty miles from here. Towards Poland, right down the Elbe. On the map it's Pardubice, but there was a village called Semtín, which Semtex – Semtín, explosive – is named after. The plant's there now instead. The plant itself is huge, a big block of concrete, surrounded by barbed wire and sentry boxes. You'd think they had something to hide!' She laughed harshly.

'Go on.'

'Don't worry,' she said nastily. 'I'm not a tease. You know that. You'll get your money's worth.'

'Sorry.' He grimaced ingratiatingly. He couldn't blow this one; he'd have to keep shtum.

'Well, when I was growing up, not just the

factory and what had been Semtín, but all of Pardubice and all up to Hradec Králové was completely out of bounds to foreigners. Give me a cigarette, will you? Thanks. That could be why I grew up with such a thing about the West; it wasn't like growing up in Prague, you see it was like growing up on a military base on the moon. The plant gave work to the town; it gave us life. My parents worked there, and my uncles and aunts and older cousins. My friends' parents. Just everyone.'

'You poor kid,' he said, unwisely.

'Listen, it's OK.' Her voice toughened up. 'Maybe it was good for me to grow up with such a graphic representation of the life I didn't want all around me. Maybe if I'd grown up here, where there are lots of things to make you want to stay, I might have grown soft. But growing up *there* ... ' Her voice trailed off and came back with all guns blazing. 'No way!' She pronounced the words with a strong, unintentional American accent, maximising the distance they put between her Czech past and her American future.

'Tell me about your parents.' He tried not to sound too much like a dirty old shrink.

'They've both worked there for ages. Since I was little. Long, long shifts – ten hours, twelve. But they never complained about their work; it's funny, plant people didn't. I think part of them was proud of what they were doing – I know that must seem monstrous to you. Semtex was called the Rolls-Royce of explosives; it was sure as hell the nearest any of *us* were going to get to a Rolls-Royce.' She drew hard on her cigarette and lifted her chin. 'Correction. Any of *them.*'

'Right,' he said smarmily.

She glared at him. 'Shut up for five minutes, can you, Gary? I'm not some dopey civilian you're trying to tap for a story. I'm a professional, too, remember? A professional Czech wannabe emigré, ever ready with my tale of woe for the oh-so-sympathetic West. She's plucky! She's fucky!! I know what you want even better than you do. So just keep it shut.'

'Right you are.' Had she ever missed one opportunity to put him down? He racked his brains, but couldn't think of one. Jesus, what would she be like as a *wife*; it made the blood run cold. Anybody bargaining for a submissive Slav slut was in for a rude awakening, green card or no green card.

She made Miranda and Nikki look like Moslem brides in comparison. Yet he liked and respected her more than any woman he'd ever known. People always swore that women loved bastards. What they didn't dare tell you was that men, the poor saps, loved beautiful female bastards twice as much.

'Where was I? Oh yeah – my enchanted childhood.' She barked with laughter, and choked on her cigarette. Serve you right, bitch. 'Well, we might have been isolated and bored in Pardubice, and there wasn't much to do in the evenings apart from put explosives through our neighbours' letterboxes, but we the people certainly obtained some measure of comfort and joy from knowing that, for once, Czechoslovakia was actually producing a *household name* – like Coca Cola, only it kills you! And we, not the smart alecs in Prague, were responsible; ah, sweet mystery of life!' She chuckled, then spoke softly, almost nostalgically. 'I don't think you can possibly understand, you see, what it felt like for a nothing little country to invent something which, time and time again, could confuse all the luscious space-age technology of the West and leave it standing; not the

Russians, even, but us! It was the one arena where we had it over the lot of you. "We are a nation of scientists," some man in a white coat said when the finger was first pointed at us, "so it is no surprise to us that Semtex is a Czechoslovakian product." ' She laughed, horribly. 'Like a child, almost; the pride in the achievement itself, no matter how murderous or immoral the achievement is. What is it we were so proud of all those years? Producing the means of murdering even more people even more efficiently, that's what – cost-effectively, too! And we didn't even have to do the job ourselves; we could leave it to the fucking Arabs.'

'Language,' said Gary automatically.

She glared at him again. 'Piss off.'

'Sorry!' he grimaced, and sought blindly to make amends. 'Listen – if you'd rather not go on – ' He tried to look as if her welfare was his one and only concern, while all the time praying that she wasn't going to take him up on this monumentally dumb offer.

'It's OK.' She shook herself like a wet dog – the image brought a lump to his groin – and when she began to speak again it was in the completely dispassionate voice of a child learning times-tables by rote. 'Semtex. Semtex is wrapped as a rule in carrot-coloured wax paper with EXPLOSIVE PLASTIC SEMTEX-H printed on. It goes out in blocks, but can be shaped anyway you like, to fit anything. Like the – ' She swallowed – 'like the bomb on the Pan Am flight over Scotland, where it was packed inside a radio and cassette player. It is so ironic, you don't think, that all these consumer beauties that we in Czechoslovakia would give anything for end up as the containers for bombs we help the Arabs make so that we can get the petro-dollars to buy radios and cassette players.' She giggled unwholesomely. 'There's got to be a better way of shopping, hasn't there? Anyway, out it goes to our brothers in the struggle in the Middle East ... '

' ... Though the Communist regime claimed they never supplied terrorists ... ' he put in eagerly.

She looked at him pityingly. 'Yes, Gary, that's right. Just Libya, South Yemen and the PLO. Them and the Moose Lodge. In 1976, it was Semtex that the scumbag put into the handbag of his pregnant girlfriend before kissing her goodbye

at the airport – she was going on holiday on an El
Al plane, you see. God! – is there a more low-
down, dirty, cowardly weapon than ours? All those
years we thought we were making a Rolls-Royce;
we were making the world's biggest hearse.' She
buried her face in her hands; a tad theatrically, he
thought, but never mind. It was one hell of a big
topic. *Topic*; he cringed inwardly. This wasn't a
topic, it was life. His reaction reminded him of a
young Oxbridge blade on the picture desk who, on
seeing a photograph of a starving child somewhere
in Africa, had shaken his head and breathed, with
tears in his eyes, 'What an incredibly striking
image.' Max, as Gary remembered, had hauled
him off and punched him. Drunk or not, it had
been a great gesture. *Gesture*; there he went again.

He gathered his thoughts and tried to bring
both himself and Maria back on track. 'And now
… ? Didn't Havel say the game was over?'

She shrugged. 'You're the journalist, Gary. It's
his job to make speeches; your job to find out if
they're true or just sweet talk.' She put out her
hand and stared boldly at him. 'Give.'

'You're kidding.' His incredulity made him forget his place. 'You've told me nothing I couldn't

get from ten minutes in a cuttings library. I wouldn't give you a handful of *halér* for that little resumé – let alone the pounds sterling you're after.'

'Dollars.' She glared at him, but without hostility. She'd basically been trying it on; she was just like him.

'Dollars, then. Or whatever Toytown crap you're after this week.'

She gurgled; she liked him piqued. Only stupid girls liked to make men jealous; smart girls preferred pique. 'So what did you want to know then, just out of curiosity?'

'I want to *know*.' He grabbed her, but gently; to show her he was serious, not to threaten he might be psychotic. 'I want to know if the stuff's still being made in those huge quantities. I want to know where it's going and who's selling it. I want to know if Havel knows. Above all I want the Semtex Story in glorious VistaVision, with no diplomatic editing to save the blushes of all our governments. I want to find out about the gap of more than three hundred metric tonnes between what left Semtin and what got to OMNIPOL, for starters. I want an in, and you can help me.'

She blinked slowly at him, then looked away as though considering whether or not to tell him something. 'You want me undercover, is that it? To put you in touch with people in Pardubice?'

He nodded eagerly.

She smiled in slow motion; one side of her mouth rising and then the other. It was a smile of triumph, but also one of complicity. He was going to hear bad news, but she was going to tell him something good anyway. 'Sorry, someone beat you to it. Undercover and under the covers.'

He was stunned, but too intrigued to feel hurt. 'Who? Who are you working for?'

'The man I love, of course.' She twinkled. 'LaMonte.'

LaMonte ...

Gary's mind began to work wildly. He was vaguely aware of Maria getting up from the bed and wandering around the room looking for her feverishly discarded clothes, like some girl in a Mittel European fairytale following a trail of breadcrumbs home to her wicked stepmother (stepfather, if you counted LaMonte Johnson), as she always did after sex and a decent interval.

For once, he wasn't interested in lying back and looking through the eyes of lust at her as she pulled on garment after garment – the lovely white stilettos always first, of course. Watching Maria put her clothes on was a million times more arousing than watching other girls take them off – even Nikki, who no matter how horny always contrived to caper around in high heels, clingtop stockings and one Eric Beamon earring before Gary gave in and hauled her on to the bed.

But now he was aroused enough already, thank you ma'am. A bit too aroused. His head swam, as though he had drunk too much bad hooch too fast. Though fast was the only way to drink bad hooch, if you thought about it.

So that was LaMonte's mysterious mission – to detonate the Semtex supply to the West and make sure the new guys in the bloc lived up to their promises. It made sense; the US didn't have a constant barrage of IRA bombs to contend with, but the Lockerbie tragedy had cut deep and there were always the Libyans to consider. It made sense to put a man on the case, to – find out if it was still being made? Being sold? Being sold by

OMNIPOL, or by the same rogue salesman who made merry with the three hundred tonnes? To snoop on Havel? To shop him? To show him proof that would make him put a stop to Semtex production once and for all? All of these?

Or none ...

In a newspaper office, conspiracy theories as much as Chivas Regal are as mother's milk to young journalists. They are drip-fed conspiracy theories by the older hacks, like farmers' wives nursing orphaned hedgehogs back to health with milk in eye-droppers, from the very first morning they enter the office, until the spark of suspicion appears in their eyes and the bloom of self-righteousness infuses their downy cheek. That is the moment, in journalism, when a boy becomes a man; when he works up his very own conspiracy theory.

And Gary had been extra lucky. He had been under the watchful eye of Max for most of his time at the *MOS*, and Max was the conquistador of the conspiracy theory. Thanks to his tutelage, Gary now felt confident that he could construct a decent-sized conspiracy theory out of one false passport, two eggboxes, a bounced cheque and a sheet or two of sticky-backed plastic, just like on *Blue Peter*.

And the great thing about CTs, Gary told himself as Maria finished dressing, is that you can be cool *and* hot; you can laugh at yourself for giving credence and even life to them, while the weight of historical evidence is behind you all the way.

For a start – let's just run it up the flagpole – how come Johnson was so damned rich? If it really was old family money as Maria claimed (the jumped-up little tart), then how come Golden Boy was over here roughing it like a working stiff? It was hardly the Ambassador to the Court of St James gig, now was it? And that phoney crap about how much he loved the country; obviously a smokescreen to provide an above-board reason for being there. No, it was much more likely that good old Monty baby worked for his money like everyone else. Or not like anyone else, as it might turn out.

How? Easy. He was CIA. Under the cover of stopping Semtex from leaving Czechoslovakia, he was actually buying it and then selling it to the Libyans for twice the price, presuming it was now rather more difficult to get hold of than it had been under the old regime. The stuff was certainly user-friendly; as bendy as bubblegum, it would fit a treat in the old diplomatic bags, which of course were never searched.

And the Vachss connection? Sure, Maria was beautiful. But as well as looking like a Tartar princess, she had all the sweet, submissive nature of one, too. If a man was seeking sanctuary from the ball-breaking bitches of Europe West, was Maria Vachss really the girl he would choose?

Of all the girls in Prague, wasn't it a happy coincidence that LaMonte Johnson had promised marriage, a green card and happy shopping at Saks Fifth Avenue ever after to the sex bomb from Semtex City herself? And her parents actually worked at the bloody plant – not one of them, but both of them! That wasn't a putative marriage; it was a proposed merger. A merger most foul.

Was he raving? He checked himself. But he didn't think so. In the past, the CIA had bagged drug crops they were meant to destroy, hadn't they? And sold them for profit, and – knowing them – pleasure. What was to stop them doing the same with Semtex? Even the great Marco Bondini had made the comparison. Marco ...

'Gary?'

He wished Maria would take herself off sharpish for once and let him go home and phone Marco. 'Yes, angel?'

'Why do you talk like that?' she said, a bit panicky. She sounded like a real Bohunk, he reflected absently.

'Like what?'

She stood in front of him, biting her lip and looking suspicious of his motives. Which was pretty much business as usual, really. She was dressed in a matte black raincoat, which for once he had absolutely no desire to tear open, and holding a manmade black shoulder bag in her hands.

'Why isn't your bag leather?' he asked her pleasantly. 'Couldn't your rich boyfriend find the readies?'

'I don't like to accept too many presents from him. You wouldn't understand. It's the same reason I wear these shoes you're so fond of mocking. It'll be different when we're married, I told him.'

'For richer, for poorer, eh?'

'What is it? Why are you looking at me like that?'

'Like what?'

'Like you're planning something. Weighing things up and coming to some nasty conclusion.'

'Sorry, sorry.' He shook himself and smiled weakly. 'I was going into major career opportunity mode. I'm not the best of company right now.'

'You want me to go, is that it? So you can get on with your investigations.'

He was about to nod sheepishly, and then thought better of it. Actually, if push came to shove he didn't want her to go, story or not. He held out his hands. 'Maria, I can't imagine ever wanting you to go.'

She wasn't having any. She stood her ground and stared him down. Then her hand dove into the bag. 'Relax. Don't sweat it. After all, now you've got your own personal clippings computer that sucks cock on the side, too.' She handed him something and slouched off to sit on the window-sill, staring at him with a bad humour.

It was a newspaper cutting; newish, and small-ish, and taking a somewhat censorious line on a suspected arms dealer who had been blown to bits by his own illegal stash of 'an explosive' in his own car. In the forest around Pardubice, which had

'once' (a nice touch, Gary thought), under the evil
Communist regime, exported murder and may-
hem all over the glorious West.

He looked up at her sharply. She sat perched
against the Prague night sky, staring at him.
'What's all this, then?' He was aware that his voice
was raw and raucous and as Cockney as it ever
got, and that he sounded quite like a stroppy
stallholder accusing his wife of screwing around.
Hardly the right tone with which to worm a brilliant story out of a nervy piece like Maria. 'I mean,
who ... '

'It's a guy I used to know.' She weaved her fingers together, put them at arm's length and
cracked them nervously.

'Fuck him, did you?' he couldn't stop himself
from leering accusingly.

She looked shocked.

'Don't answer that,' he said hastily. Now was
obviously not the time for moral tutorials or post-
dated jealousies.

'Yes, I will answer it, dammit!' She was incan-
descently irritated. 'And no, I did not sleep with
this man!' Her voice was high and indignant. 'It
may surprise you, Gary, as you so obviously

believe me to be a total whore, but I never "fucked", as you put it, one single man, boy or dog from Pardubice. Gustav – which is the name of this dead person – went to the same school as I did, although he was three or so years ahead of me. Chronologically, that is. Intellectually he was light years behind. He was the first person from Pardubice I knew who moved to Prague. That's all. Gustav the Groover, he used to call himself.'

'Go on.'

'I'm going, I'm going. Well, he used to hang out with those awful hippie dissident rock bands here; he used to come back to Pardubice about once a month to visit his mother. He always brought her masses of things – food, clothes, then electronic consumer durables; don't laugh at me, Gary!'

'I wasn't.' He pulled his face straight with a real effort.

'You were.' She frowned, and cracked her fingers again. 'Well, Gustav was obviously making a lot of money in Prague. And most people in Pardubice believed he was a drug dealer.'

'Can he get me a gram of coke?' Gary cracked lamely.

'No, he can't. Because he's dead. And if you shut up for five minutes, I'll tell you why.'

'Sorry.'

'A couple of years ago, Gustav moved back in with his mother. Into her cramped little flat in Pardubice! – well, everyone thought he was crazy, his mother most of all. She barely had room for herself, let alone Gustav – they'd moved her to a tiny widow's flat, you see. As I say, crazy; if you were living in Prague and making good money, everyone said, why on earth would you want to move back to a one whore town – '

'One horse town,' he said automatically.

'You obviously don't know Pardubice, darling.' She gave him A Look. 'Horses we have plenty of – but only one whore.'

He decided to keep his mouth shut. It would, as she had told him, make life so much more simple.

' – to a one whore town like Pardubice? Doesn't add up. Well, one evening I told LaMonte about him – just in passing, like "Isn't this strange?" type of thing. And LaMonte asked me if he could meet him – Gustav. I said I would arrange a meeting.'

'And then?'

She shrugged. 'And I did.'

'And now this guy – Groovy Gustav – ' He was almost stuttering.

'And now this guy appears to have moved from dealing drugs to peddling explosives. With which, presumably, he blew himself up.'

'Do you know how difficult it is to blow yourself up with Semtex?' He was off the bed now and grabbing her, not so much in anger as excitement. 'Do you? Of course you do. You know that you can hold a butt-naked flame next to Semtex and it won't explode. The only way to make that stuff go off is to detonate it – make it into a bomb. And would this Gustav the Groover have made a bomb up in his car? The whole point about Semtex is that you sell it straight and it's so malleable it can be smuggled out in anything. Then you make it into a bomb, once it's through customs.' He was gabbling now, and digging his fingers into her arms until she squealed.

'Gary!'

'I'm sorry – I'm sorry!' He released her and walked back across the room, still naked, his hand to his forehead. 'My God, oh my God – *this is my story, this is my story*! Your boyfriend – he blew old Gustav the Groover up! Sweet as a nut!'

'So?' She lifted her head and stuck out her chin. 'He was selling Semtex. He dealt in death. He deserved it.'

'Sure.' He nodded brightly. 'Whatever you like. I'm not a social worker, as you've always taken great delight in pointing out to me. I'm a low-down dirty hack with the morals of a – well, a Czech.'

She swore, exotically.

'But don't you see what a great story it is? In the new, free Czechoslovakia, under the sinister shadow of the Carpathian mountains yet in the domain of the New World Order – you've got your light and your shade, see; very important in radio – the CIA and the Commies still do battle unto the death! It's beautiful – James Bond out of Lord Reith!'

'Except for the inconvenient fact that Gustav wasn't a Communist, but a hippie hustler.' She narrowed her eyes. 'And that LaMonte Johnson is certainly not CIA.'

'Oh yeah?' He was limboing into his clothes like greased lightning. 'Tell that to the Marines. If your darling Semtex hasn't blown them up yet.' Thanks, Marco. 'And I'll tell you what – ' He buckled his belt with one hand and pointed evangelically at her with the other. 'Not only would I bet my last *halér* that your boyfriend's CIA, but that he's bent CIA to boot.'

'What the hell are you talking about?' She sprang up and stalked over to him.

'Act your age, Miss Vachss. As you were forever saying to me.'

'That's odd – I don't remember ever calling you Miss Vachss. Not even at our weirdest.'

'In a manner of speaking.' He spoke impatiently. 'Look. You said yourself that Gustav the Groover sold drugs before he sold Semtex. Well, the CIA used to bag drugs from dealers under the cover of law and order and then sell them themselves – exactly what's to stop them doing the same with Semtex?'

She was silent for a moment, considering it. And they said loyalty was dead! 'But I can't see why ... why he would jeopardise his position in this way. With his money already, from his family ... '

'Seen any snapshots of them, babes? Mom, Pop, dogs, stately pile in Washington?'

She looked confused. 'No ... but ... '

'Take it from me.' He pulled on his shoes. 'Old

money my ass. Your old boyfriend's money's even younger than you are.' He stood up. 'It's about as old as the so-called Semtex ban. Which did nothing but drive the price of the ugly fucking stuff straight through the ceiling. And right into your boyfriend's bank account.'

She sat down on the bed, looking shocked. He had a sudden urge to feed her hot, sweet tea – preferably through his penis. He sat down and put an arm around her. 'Come on. It's not the end of the world.'

'Damn right it isn't.' She jumped to her feet, pulling the tight belt of her raincoat even tighter. 'Not the end of my world. I'm getting out of here – with a king, a cop or a killer, I don't give a damn. But it could be the end of yours, if you find out too much and tell it to the wrong people. See you around, sucker – if the CIA don't see you first.'

And with a swirl and a slam, she was gone.

12

Gary sat at his desk sipping black coffee. He hated the taste of it. But then he hated the taste of everything these days. When he could taste anything. He felt as though he'd had mumps. Well, he had, but not recently.

A pile of old newspaper clippings – courtesy of the World Service library – had been pushed aside. All night he'd crouched over the yellowing pages waiting to pounce upon any piece of useful information; all he got were a few crumbs of biography and a creased picture of a dapper LaMonte at an Embassy reception, making Mrs Temple Black and Mr Havel laugh.

Ha fucking ha, he thought; lover boy won't be laughing for long. In the background he could just make out Maria; was it a grin or a grimace on that beautiful face? Waving, drowning or drunk? Whichever, he bet she'd been singularly hot in the sackeroo that particular night. There was nothing like mixing high to get Maria Vachss horny. The thought that she had a past, as well as a future, without him made Gary suddenly sick with jealousy; he felt a bitter wave of coffee come perilously close to his palate. And here in his hands was a snapshot of her future, a life sentence of small talk and mandatory smiles – his Maria, the trophy wife, trailing behind the tall man in the tuxedo. Maria Johnson? – she's charming. Apparently he found her when he was doing his stretch in Czechoslovakia.

He tried to tell himself it wasn't all entirely personal; he was a professional journalist, just doing his job. A total lie, of course – his hatred of LaMonte had become as intense as his passion for Maria.

A girlfriend Gary had given the shove had said, the stuffy cow, 'I feel sorry for you, Gary. You'll never know what love is. And love is the one thing that could ever make you a better man than you are.' (He'd tried to keep a straight face.) 'Go on, you bastard, laugh. You're the loser, not me.' The door had slammed right on cue. He was tempted to call her up – Shari, Charlotte, what was her name? No matter. But if he did have her name and number to hand, he'd call her up right this minute and tell the stupid cow that yes, he'd finally experienced this zing called love. And hand in hand with it, something he'd never really known before; hatred. Pure, passionate hatred, the kind that produces those sick daydreams of doing real and lasting damage to someone. Love had not made him a better man at all. It had made him desperate. And dangerous.

If he could nail Johnson all his problems would be solved. Finish LaMonte and his future was secure. But what if he was wrong? What if Johnson was guilty of nothing more than being middle-aged and in love with Maria. (And blowing up some Semtex-dealing scum, but that was more of a social service than a crime.) What if the only evidence he could come up with was his own battered ego? Your Honour, this man broke my heart – for that he deserves the death penalty!

'Enough!' Gary shouted aloud, startling himself and then slapping himself around the face. The only antidote to his feverish fantasies were facts.

He looked at the photograph again, hoping for an everyday miracle or a smudge of evidence. He brought it closer to his eyes, then laughed – what was he looking for, a 666 or two little horn buds either side of the guy's forehead? He sighed and put the picture down, smoothing it with his hands. Back to basics, boy. Step One – Know Your Subject. But how?

Max! The name popped up like a password to a computer screen.

Gary looked at his watch. It was three in the morning; too late to call most mortals, but not Max, who was something either less or more than human – what was it? Probably both.

Gary could picture him now, in that flat of his in Vauxhall, hunched over his keyboard, babbling to himself like a baby, crooning to himself like a mother, swigging back his Rebel Yell miniatures ('Just the one!'); with his fidgety fingers he'd tiptoe through the tulips and into the data banks of the world and beyond, taking whatever he fancied. Or what he thought his friends might like.

Gary had once spent a night in the London office, mesmerised, watching Max at work; it had been a virtuoso performance of high-tech hustle and heroic chutzpah. He'd be talking to someone in North America on the phone, faxing someone in Japan and plugging into a plethora of Kraut computers – all at once.

Gary thought of himself as a guy who occasionally walked on the wild side – taking care to be home before daybreak, of course. He realised after meeting Max that he was still in his pram. He'd seen a lot of young journos who thought that a crate of Bud made them into real gone gonzo geezers. But Max made Hunter S. Thompson look like Alistair Cooke. He'd pace around swilling tequila and bourbon chased by Carlsberg Special Brew, sniffing long snaking lines of sulphate and coke; he called it 'getting psyched up'. To Gary it had looked like a very enjoyable suicide. Then, too tense to work, Max would try to 'cool out' with huge quantities of cough syrup. Then he'd complain that he was too relaxed – 'chilled' – to work.

And start all over again.

But it seemed to work. By 3 a.m. Max would be pumping, pounding the keyboard, staring at the screen with bug eyes and blood pouring from his nose – 'For God's sake, Max! At least mop it up! You'll electrocute yourself!' 'You mop it up for me, candy ass! I'm cooking!' – hacking his way into the heart of darkness, hoping and dreaming and praying that he might shed light on the darkest secrets of industrialists, fascists, corrupt cartels, intelligence agencies and men who wore tasselled loafers. In the new and growing global village, he was the info-idiot who really knew what was going on. The rich and the powerful could run, and they could hide, and they could have plastic surgery – but sooner or later they would hear from Max.

Max was a phone freak, wedded for life like a nun. He boasted of his collection of telephone numbers the way other men bragged of notches on their belts.

'Go on. Who would you like to talk to? The Prime Minister, the Queen? Bush, the Pope?

Madonna? Go on, name one. I got their number.'
Max had sat back, smug, and twirled his card
index happily.

'You're joking.'

Max looked aggrieved, as if his manhood had
been called into question. 'Come on. I'll fucking
show you. Who do you want – Pope frigging John
Paul? Princess Di? Georgie Bush? Yeah, let's give
El Presidento a buzz.' Max leaned forward in his
whirly chair and twirled his index with intent.

'Max, you can't just call the President of the
United States out of the blue!'

'Why not? We have the technology. Once power
came from learning the secrets of the natural
world, and from that we created modern technology. But now power comes from learning the
secrets of modern technology itself. The
combinations, the sequences of numbers, codes,
passwords. People phone the President all the
time. The trick is to know the code that connects
you straight to his personal line.'

Max picked up the receiver, cuddled it to his
neck with his chin, placed a bourbon miniature to
his lips, sucking on it like a baby, and closed his
eyes. One long nicotined finger leaped out as if it

had a life of its own, tapped out a series of numbers and returned to its master.

Max listened for a second and then reeled off a short sequence of numbers. Then he smiled, and handed Gary the phone.

'Yes,' a weary American voice said. It sounded like a command.

Gary opened his mouth, and froze that way. As though he was a child, and the wind had changed.

'Go on,' hissed Max.

'Mr President?' Gary squeaked.

'Yes?' impatiently.

That was enough. Gary slammed the phone down and kept his hand on it. He was panting. 'Fuck me.'

Max grinned.

Yes, if there was even a speck of dirt in LaMonte's past then Max could deliver it at the flick of a switch – assuming, that was, that it was the right kind of dirt; professional, covert dirt done in the name of democracy. Max always said that it was the hidden stuff that was the easiest to zero in on; semi-exposed scandals got lost in the headlines.

And of course, Max's magnificent obsession, the subject of the book he'd been 'researching' for the last ten years, was the CIA.

When people called him a crazy conspiracy freak, Max invariably countered with the claim that the idea of the crazy conspiracy freak was itself a CIA conspiracy. Gary thought he was a trifle touched, yet he had always felt a sort of envy for Max; to care that much, to be consumed by a cause. It was the difference between writing copy and waging a crusade.

Because beneath all of Max's crazy talk was a real concern for something more than deadlines; a belief that there really were bad guys out there, schoolyard bullies who were somehow astride the world, and who shouldn't be allowed to get away with it. Well, now he was like that too. One of the crazies the older journalists had warned him about.

Hearing Max's voice on the phone was like hearing an old, loved pop song – an echo of his past when he had been Gaz the Lad, always in control and on the move. Now he was Gary the Geek, stumbling around in the present as though it was a foreign country, without a clue.

'Max?'

'Gazza!' As a phone addict, Max had an acute ear for voices and claimed he could detect an identity even from a cough through the telephone wire. 'How goes it? How's the Prague pussy?'

'O.K.' Time was when he would have dished the anatomical dirt and no messing. But the thought of talking about Maria like that made him shudder. He'd leave that to her legal, decent and honest fiancé. 'Listen, M. I want you to do me a favour.'

'Name it, name it.' Max loved little more than an excuse to go a-hunting. He did conspiracy favours the way disc jockeys played requests.

'I want you to run a name through your dirty tricks file – an American, known as LaMonte Johnson. Could be CIA.'

'Just a ticketyboo.' Max sprang into action, flattered and intrigued. The quickest way to Max's heart was through his data bank.

There was a remote silence, punctuated only by the tap of computer keys. Then Gary heard a receiver being picked up clumsily, dropped, sworn at and picked up again.

'OK ... get ready ... yes, yes ... come on, baby ... yes, looks like we have a little something for you here!' Max was cooking. Gary heard a miniature lose its lid.

'What? What?' He knew Max enjoyed making people wait, building the tension. It wasn't sadism, but the arrogance of the artiste.

'Well, I'll give you just a little taste now – ' Max took a swig of bourbon ' – and fax you the rest soonest. LaMonte Johnson, real name so far as we can tell, born in ... Nebraska. Father a farmer. Won a scholarship to Harvard, early Sixties, to study politics ... spied on student activists for the FBI. Oh-oh, we got us a weirdo; actually volunteered for Vietnam. Failed fitness; joined CIA. Junior official counter-terrorism. In the Seventies moved to Washington; policy units, think-tanks. Joined diplomatic corps – started out in Latin America and then to Czechoslovakia. Clean noses all round, for a dirty tricks man. In short, a real poor boy made bad.'

'How bad?'

'You want this guy, yeah?' Max gurgled luxuriously. 'Yeah, you want him bad. Well, it's hard to say – I'll have to dig a little deeper. But my guess would be – um, minor league player, cool, competent but not a major-major crazy.' Max whooped. 'Not like me!'

'Max, have you heard anything untoward concerning the CIA and Semtex?' He kept his voice low, despite the time and the space.

'Sure – but then I've heard things untoward concerning the CIA and Play-Doh. But yeah – some of them would like nothing more than to get their paws on the sticky stuff. And not to make models.'

'Why?' His throat was dry. He wished he had a bourbon miniature to hand.

'There's been … ah, talk of Semtex killings by the CIA to keep Gaddafi in the headlines. Little things. The Cold War's over, and the boys need a baddy if they want to keep their gigs.'

'Do you believe this? Serious?'

'Man, I've been studying these guys for longer than I like to dwell on.' Max's voice was nostalgic, almost romantic. 'And one thing I've learned; the more crazy it sounds, the more likely it's true.'

'Max, thanks. No. I don't know how to thank you – '

'I got a way.'

Gary prepared himself for some obscene request. 'Name it.'

'Just be careful, buddy. These guys play to win. And they don't give a fuck who they have to take out to do it.'

'Got you.' Gary heard Max bang down the receiver in London. He hung up slowly. 'I've got you,' he said again, slowly. But this time he wasn't talking to his friend.

13

Gary sipped from his cold cup of milky coffee and experienced the vile sensation of pulling out its skin on his lower lip. It hung there, triumphantly repulsive, until he wiped it off. He sighed, rolled the soiled tissue into a ball, dropped it on the café table and picked up his Game Boy for the umpteenth time that day.

It was his day off, and he was spending it playing Nintendo and wiping coffee skin off his face in a public place because that public place gave a very good view of the Schönborn Palace. Occasionally, to break the monotony, he would leap up, sending crockery flying, when the sinister silhouette of LaMonte Johnson showed itself in the doorway of the Palace, and follow him, hopefully unseen. So far today they had accompanied each other, at a distance, to a flower shop on Moskevská and the Indická restaurant on Štěpánská, both times to no avail. The Tetris blocks on his Game Boy tormented him as they fell, with a little fine-tuning, neatly into place. If only life was like a game of Tetris – he'd be a bloody Grandmaster by now! Here was this weird guy who had CIA written all over him, who was a damn sight richer than he ought to be and who had apparently bumped off some arms dealer in the forests of Semtín, no doubt after stealing the booty Gustav the Gormless had brought to sell to the American.

But how the Sam Hill was he ever going to prove it – short of catching the guy red-handed, or brown-handed as the case may be. Short of his premium bond coming up, being able to give up working for a living, offering Maria his hand and a massive pre-marital settlement and getting her to rifle through the Yank's diplomatic bags. But then, if he was rich enough not to work he wouldn't *need* the ruddy story in the first place.

(A patent lie. He was the sort of airhead who, had he been born rich, would have felt it necessary to slog even harder for recognition in his own right. It was becoming very clear very quickly to Gary First that he was not the straightforward lad about town he had always liked to think himself.)

So what were his other chances, the least he could get to go on with? He had to see Johnson handing over money to someone. Or vice versa. Either way looked pretty bloody suspicious. But would Johnson do it himself? Wouldn't he send some Embassy lackey to do his dirty work? The answer came back loud and clear; not if he was bent, self-serving CIA (though wouldn't any alternative type be an honest to God oxymoron?) Then he would have to do every last schlepp himself, which made this eternal, infernal waiting well within earshot of the call of duty. Worse luck.

But what was this? Gary's knee shot up, sending the coffee's sediment spluttering all over his Game Boy. He looked around wildly, and finding nothing else wiped the precious machine right down the front of his white Reporter jacket. Clothes you could just about buy in Prague; Nintendo for less than a limb, not yet.

It was LaMonte Johnson; cool as a courgette (cucumbers were far too common) and stepping out of the Schönborn Palace. Only this time – *this* time – he was carrying a whopping great black briefcase which could easily have been borrowed from the props department of a John Le Carré film. It was a briefcase born to be handed to a bad man, preferably containing large and illicit quantities of readies, moolah or spondulicks. Something Nasty In the Briefcase had replaced Something Nasty In The Woodshed in modern novels, and Gary could see why looking at this black beast. It was the Briefcase From Hell.

He thrust some *halér* at the disgruntled babushka behind the counter – racist, ageist, sexist stereotype, he noted with the *Journalist's Handbook* side of his mind – and skidded into the street. There the cocky bastard was – strolling past the police station that the Communists had so thoughtfully installed next to the Schönborn Palace when it became the US Embassy. Look at him, not a care in the world – first, second or

Third – his briefcase swinging, to the end of Tržiště. He turned into Karmelitská; now Gary moved, bustling to the corner and peering carefully around it.

He saw Johnson walk past the strange and beautiful Vrtba Gardens, laid out in 1720 and topped with the unearthly observation terrace and its sad Baroque statues – he didn't try the gate, as was the habit of all hopeful Westerners walking down this street. A man in a hurry, if not a worry. Past the Church of Our Lady of Victory. (What, not going to light a candle for Gustav the Gormless?)

Gary only moved into Karmelitská when Johnson turned left down Harantova, to come out in front of the Embassy of the Netherlands. Did he have business there, perhaps? With those peaceful Lowlanders? Not very likely.

But hush, hush, whisper who dares – there was the delicately Rococo Turba Palace, where the salary men of the Japanese diplomatic corps laid their futons and their customised bottles of Glenmorangie. And – Buddha on a bicycle – LaMonte Johnson, now swinging that bulging briefcase like there was no tomorrow (which there wouldn't be, for him, if Gary played his cards right) was going right through the front door. Gary dodged back around the corner in Karmelitská, and leaned against the wall to light a gasper. It was a cliché, to follow someone *and* smoke, but he had decided for the moment to yield to the luxurious mindless pleasure of living a cliché.

Japan! He inhaled sharply. It was weird – but, from a conspiracy theory point of view, absolutely perfect. The Japanese were the Americans' real enemy, beneath all the war stories in the Middle East; it was they who had hit the very foundations of the American Dream. Only they could pay a rogue CIA male the sort of money he dreamed of, now Communism was gone and Islam was on the run.

The Japanese ... they had been hated, for all the wrong reasons, by America throughout the Eighties and the Nineties so far; seen their imports burned and their intentions blamed. They would be barely human if they didn't start to hate back sooner or later. They were rich, as few countries were rich now; yet loathe ever to go to war again. Semtex in the hands of hired killers might prove the perfect way to strike back against a jealous, jeering world; especially if they should ever want to hit America where it hurt. If China could bankroll the PLO, why not Japan the Libyans? It was a cinch! A wrap! The End Of America! No, make that Amerikkka!

He put his head back round the corner only to see Johnson, briefcase intact, whistling past the sunken arcade which led to the Prague Conservatoire. A bilious cantata of grunts and squeals floated from there into Harantova; Gary knew just how they felt.

Johnson turned into Maltese Square and Gary moved stealthily along to the restaurant on the corner of Harantova. It had once been a popular eating place for *le tout* Prague; since 1991, when it had been taken over by French management, the local experience of the place was limited to reading the menu, stuck callously in the window and changed every day, and calculating how many days' work it would take to raise the price of an avocado starter.

Turn right out of Maltese Square, and there were the two much-restored Gothic towers of the Church of Our Lady Under the Chain – crazy name, but the place was always closed. Right again, keeping well back, by the Musical Instrument Museum. The American's pace slowed here. Maybe old Monty baby was out for nothing more low-down and dirty than a jam.

No; he was turning left now, into verdant Grand Prior's Square. Here was the apricot and white French Embassy; and here, surely, was the end of the journey. For the French, of all people, were never averse to blowing people up – especially innocent people. The bombing of the *Rainbow Warrior*, manned by fellow Europeans in the friendly port of New Zealand, filled Gary's mind. You want cowardly, creepy acts of terrorism, tailor-made for the Semtex style? The French had 'em, in spades. A fading power in a permanent panic over its place in the world; it had to be.

But would you credit it? The Yank was moving on, past the John Lennon Wall! Absorbed in his schmoozing as he was, Gary felt compelled to take a moment out to contemplate the John Lennon Wall, which must surely have been the most objectionable creation in Prague – apart from LaMonte Johnson himself, of course.

The wall was a graffiti artist's nightmare. The

Czechs liked to think of themselves as the most sophisticated of all the Europe Easters, so far as Gary could see. But this had not stopped them from swallowing whole – right down the windpipe – the moronic myth of Saint John the Beatle Martyr.

After the crooner's murder in 1980 (Gary remembered well where he had been; in bed, asleep, waking with a jolt of dismay when his mother's anguished bleat of 'They've shot Lennon!' shattered the fervent calm of their semi. He had felt a distinct pang of sorrow – but only because he thought she meant Lemmon, Jack Lemmon, whose suits he had admired in many a black and white film. When he found out it was that whining four-eyes his parents had worshipped as flaming youngbloods, he'd said, 'Thank God!' His parents had merely looked at each other, confirmed once again in their suspicion that they had Raised A Monster. He'd only been about thirteen at the time, but he reckoned he had shown remarkably mature judgement), the wall had become a site of battle by spraypaint between a large part of Prague's social element and the police. The youth would come out under the cover of night and cover the wall in half-assed and hypocritical slogans – GIVE PEACE A CHANCE! – before going on to kick seven shades of shit out of each other, as was their wont and national sport. And the likely lads of the VB would wheel up the next day with a paddywagon full of whitewash and do the decent thing. At the height of the struggle, video surveillance gear was installed and trained on the wall, which probably merely served to encourage the dumb clucks even further; they most likely thought they'd end up as the token Gritty Black and White Video From Exotic Yerp on their darling MTV ...

When a goodish number of Prague's leading boho lights were given government gigs in 1989, the wailers at the Wall thought it was free for all time. But by 1990, the VB boys were back in force. Still, every December 8 a huge be-in took place there, as all Prague's disaffected youth cults from punks to hippies gathered to spend the night imagining no possessions before going off to mug some tourist for his running shoes.

Gary watched LaMonte follow the wall on to the bridge over the Čertovka. The so-called Devil's Stream, a tributary of the Vltava, had allegedly been named in honour of the foul temper of a washerwoman who had lived nearby. (He wondered idly if she had been a forbear of Maria's.)

Maria ... There, on the other side of the stream, was the blue eighteenth-century summerhouse which was without doubt the most coveted habitat in all of the beautiful city. Only Maria hated it (just to be interesting, probably. Or perhaps not); 'It looks like a whorehouse with frostbite. Give me a slum in Chicago anytime.'

Johnson walked on to tiny Kampa Island and through the narrow passage beyond. Gary hung back until he saw the man turn right, then followed. Johnson came out into a beautiful tree-filled square, lined with graceful, decaying Baroque houses and ending in the Gothic arches of the Charles Bridge.

It was so beautiful, and Gary's eyes were so torn between tracking Johnson and taking it all in, that he didn't even notice the window cleaner – twelve foot ladder and all. Just like in a Jack Lemmon film, the ladder hit the sharply dressed klutz full in the face as the toothless old artisan carrying it swung around to greet a friend.

The blow knocked him flat. But it didn't knock

the breath out of him; he used that, lying flat on his back, to bellow the loudest 'OH, FUCK!' that Prague had ever heard.

The window cleaner, a typical Eastern European, was beetling off like a ballistic missile, not waiting to see which way the wind of blame was blowing. But for the rest, Gary was the object of a good deal of attention; the square had excellent acoustics, and his voice carried further than he would ever have thought possible.

And here, turning back from the Charles Bridge, making an unwelcome return in his starring role as Good Samaritan with Semtex, was LaMonte Johnson, a look of apparently genuine concern clouding his face.

'Gary!' He squatted down beside him, the camel-hair coat trailing in the dust. What a regular fucking Joe he was. 'Are you OK?'

'I'm fine, fine.'

'That was some knock you took there – hey, where the hell does that guy think he's going?' LaMonte got to his feet and started after the window cleaner, obviously intent on putting a bit of his deep and sincere respect for the Czech people into action. 'Hey, you! You with the lethal ladder!'

'No!' The English loathing of Making A Fuss led Gary to rise unwisely to his feet and to overcome his natural repulsion for his girlfriend's boyfriend enough to put a restraining hand on his arm. *'Please.'*

'You sure?'

'Positive.'

LaMonte gave him a sly look. 'Ya mean ya got AIDS?' He cracked up. 'Sorry. Sick joke.'

Gary rewarded him for his humility with a watery smile.

LaMonte looked suddenly at his watch. 'Jeez, that the time? Listen, I'd love to go for a drink, make sure you're OK and all that, but I have to meet someone.' He looked around and pointed. 'You want to go in there and have a beer, and I'll meet you there after a while?'

Gary clutched his head. 'I feel weird,' he improvised. 'I'd really prefer not to be alone right now. I know this must be a drag, but it's this city – I guess I'm a bit phobic after what happened to me by the Holy Trinity that night. If I fainted around here, they'd have my hubcaps in minutes. Can't I come with you, just until my head clears? It's my day off – I don't have to be anywhere. And

I won't be any trouble to you. We could have lunch – ?' Gary took his chance.

'Listen – I'll put you in a cab. How's that sound?'

'Please, LaMonte.' Gary tried to make his voice as whiney and Limey little-boy-in-big-city as possible; not a difficult order. 'I'm real sorry to pull this one on you – but you said we could maybe help each other out … ?'

The older man's eyes looked long and hard into Gary's face, and Gary just knew that he was calculating exactly how weak and easily led the young man was. Gary got the distinct impression that a weak character would be more acceptable to the American than a strong one, and did his very best to make himself look slack-jawed, weak-chinned, weepy-eyed and generally a pushover for any strong-mind Nietzschean type who might be in the vicinity.

'Come on,' LaMonte Johnson said finally. 'But if you say a word about what you see – '

'I'm a dead man, right?' Gary tried to twinkle. This was it! What a sucker!

'Eventually. And slowly.' Johnson turned his back, dusted off his coat and picked up The Briefcase. 'Come on.'

They went on together past the last two house signs before the bridge; the dinky blue fox chewing a twig, and the Madonna between two mangle rollers.

'What does the Madonna between the mangle rollers mean?' Gary asked, playing up to his wide-eyed innocent role.

LaMonte shook his head impatiently. 'It's a long story.' He was obviously preoccupied. Then they were on the Charles Bridge itself; the curving, streamlined heartbeat of the city. Coronations, fiestas and rebellions had all been squeezed into existence through this ancient birth channel.

'Thirty statues of saints you can count along this bridge,' said LaMonte, his mood lightening. 'Some of the senior citizens still stop to lift their hats to them thirty times each and every morning.' He laughed. 'It's a better excuse than most for being late to work, I guess.'

'I heard that some of them were only copies of the originals.' From your affianced wife, actually. Apres shtup.

'That's so. The oldest is the big bronze Crucifixion there. Pretty neat, huh?'

Only an American would describe a huge bronze representation of the Crucifixion as 'pretty neat,' Gary thought smugly. Correction; only a *white trash* American! An American who had *made his own money*. If LaMonte was Ivy League, then Gary was Ivy Benson. And her All Girl Band.

LaMonte chuckled. 'Apparently your Queen Elizabeth One was pretty outraged by the size of his dong.'

Gary crowed inwardly. Come on, you crass fuck, start telling Polish jokes! I'll have you tried on grounds of taste and decency, if nothing else!

'And see that guy?'

Gary strained towards the statue, anticipating yet another good ole boy dead giveaway.

'That's St John Nepomuk. If ever anyone suspects you of doing something you didn't, he's the guy you ask for help clearing your name.' LaMonte looked at him archly and gave the slightest smile. 'And there's my man. Come on. And don't speak until you're spoken to.'

Gary all but gasped. If the man LaMonte was looking at had been sent from Central Europe Casting, he could not have been better suited to the role of down-at-heel arms dealer. His cadaverous face imploded into the turned up collar of a khaki trenchcoat, and he had the unmistakeable once-tested, always-invested Horrible Haircut of the ex-soldier. He drew deeply on his cigarette when he saw LaMonte in a way that struck Gary as almost sexual – parasexual, perhaps. (A parasexual paratrooper, heh heh.) Then he stared rudely at Gary – as though he was the Ugly Best Friend to LaMonte's Pretty Date – and turned to empty his lungs over the bridge before walking across to a bench set back from the main thoroughfare.

The meeting place, though public, made perfect sense. Probably because it *was* so public; so many millions of people crossed the Charles Bridge every day that no-one would dream of doing anything illicit there.

LaMonte started towards the bench; Gary followed him. LaMonte sat down next to the sleazy type; Gary sat next to LaMonte. LaMonte offered and lit him a cigarette, took one for himself and then, apparently as a courteous afterthought, offered one to the sleaze. '*Jak se máte*, Karlov?' said the American quietly. How are you, Gary translated to himself.

'I'm OK.' The bloody-minded bugger talked back in English, roughly. 'But who is this?'

'My young friend. New boy at the Embassy.'

Karlov darted a look of extreme mistrust at Gary. The guy was obviously a good judge of character, sleazebag or not. 'What you bring him for?'

'He's fine. One of us. Don't worry.'

'Huh.' The man put a hand on the case and stood up, taking it with him. 'OK. Cheers. Be seeing you soonest.'

'Next week, same time, same place.'

The sleaze shuffled off and LaMonte leaned back on the bench, looking out over the water. He seemed very relaxed. 'Lovely day, isn't it?'

Gary could bear it no longer. 'What was in that case?'

The American's eyes were mocking. 'Why don't you go and find out? It's not locked.' He lifted an eyebrow and smiled indulgently. 'Run along now. Or he'll be gone. There are a million stories on Charles Bridge – and you're about to lose yours.'

Throwing caution to the wind, Gary got to his feet and ran after the man. Towards the far end of the bridge he saw him and dived through the crowd, catching him by the greasy sleeve and swinging him round. 'Mr Johnson says – ' he panted. 'Got to check – could be wrong case – '

Taking advantage of the man's temporary surprise, he wrenched away the case, put it on the ground and popped both its locks. Then he gasped.

Cigarettes. A huge briefcase filled to the brim with cigarettes. American cigarettes. Hundreds of American cigarettes in shrink-wrapped boxes. Kools, Capris, Camels, Virginia Slims and Kims, Chesterfields, Marlboros and menthol Mistys, which was a new one on Gary. Cigarettes.

'Cigarettes,' he said, stunned.

'Cigarettes,' repeated LaMonte Johnson, towering above him. 'OK, Karlov, take it away. Everything would appear to be in order here.'

Karlov squatted down beside Gary and gave him an evil look as he put his booty back together. Then with an 'I go now' he was shuddering off at top speed, fearful of further delay in his pressing plans to smoke himself stupid.

'Cigarettes,' said Gary once more.

'Get up, why don't you?' the American suggested. 'Yes, cigarettes. American cigarettes. Like manna from heaven here – even to the civilised Czech. Imagine how the bums feel about them!'

'Karlov – he's a tramp?'

'Nah, he's the guy who looks after the tramps of Prague. There's an amazing number of homeless here now, since the end of the state housing subsidies. The soup kitchens keep their stomachs lined – but nobody will give the poor bastards cigarettes. Not even a Start, let alone a smooth American smoke. Those health fascists are everywhere you look these days.'

'So you – '

'Get up, will you?' LaMonte said testily.

Gary scrambled to his feet.

'So I filch 'em from the Embassy. A package of Kims from a steno, a pack of Marlboro from the muscle. In a week I can fill that case, the place is so big and the supplies are so good. And barely anyone smokes there any more anyway – they just leave them lying around for the guests. I'd rather the poor people of Prague were having a smoke on me than some fruity French diplo with a little cat's asshole for a mouth on him.'

Gary barely heard him. The shame. The sorrow. Oh, the horror, the horror.

'Am I not one great guy?' LaMonte winked lewdly. 'And a helluva fuck, too. Or so I'm told.'

Die, rich scum. Oh, die.

'Come on, let's go and get that lunch you were talking about. I could eat a horse. And, this being Europe, I probably will.'

'Sorry. I've lost my appetite.' He moved fast, head down, off the Charles Bridge. And behind him he could hear the sound of confident American laughter.

14

'**H**ello?'

'Hi, Gary. It's me.'

'MARIA!' He looked in the mirror, checked his hair and felt stupid.

'Yes, the one and only.' She sounded weary. 'Vachss the slash. Listen – talk to Marilyn.'

'Who?'

'Marilyn.' Her voice seemed to drag its feet. 'She's an alleged singer at a club called the Cashbox on Wenceslas. She was Gustav's girl – chick.

Lady. Whatever. Anyway, talk to her.'

'Thanks.' He felt his hands tighten around the receiver, attempting vainly to squeeze out every drop of her. 'But why ... ?'

'My mother went to Gustav's funeral in Pardubice. My mother is one tough broad.' She laughed arrogantly, revelling in her mother's bolshiness. It made him swoon with love. 'But she came home crying. His mother ... well, he was only a child.' She corrected herself. 'An only child.'

He felt very emotional. 'I see,' he said softly.

'I doubt it,' she snapped, and hung up.

The best thing about the Cashbox was its name. Beyond the neon sign, it had marginally less style, leg room and joie de vivre than the Central Line during rush hour. An unappetising mix of hopeless young hippies and desperate businessmen drank bad French wine and paid real money for the privilege of sticking baby laxative up their noses. While on the ever-shifting stage one of the strangest shows Gary had ever seen took place.

The girl who called herself Marilyn looked a lot like Madonna. This was partly because she had blondined her hair, but badly, and wore like medals of honour a jerry-built zinc brassiere of conical mode, laddered fishnet tights and suspenders. She wore them grimly and determinedly, like her role model; not frivolously, as Nature had intended. But mostly because she was facially the closest approximation to the Metatextual Girl he had ever seen; the nose was shorter, the eyes were bigger and brown, but that was it.

And without the trappings of her tax bracket, without the princess-and-the-pea mattress of her myth, without the enforced soft focus of the stadiums it was quite shocking to see and to comprehend exactly how plain the most famous sex symbol in the world was. All through the unhappy medium of her female impersonator here.

A bored drummer hit his drums sporadically. A saxophonist posed with his terminally posable instrument. They both looked as if they were thinking about picking up their dry cleaning tomorrow. But the safety net of a taped backing track played, and Marilyn capered, utilising every inch of the shifting stage.

Gary stood back, lit a cigarette, and gave himself up to the music. It was entertaining, but, he suspected, not in the way it was meant to be.

The girl Marilyn had studied her idol's work closely enough not to make any obvious bloomers – she did not claim to feel like a sturgeon or a surgeon, for instance, as other parodists had. But little ones had got away, to Gary's great delight. *Dress You Up*, for instance, had become a paean to group sex as Marilyn insisted that she would dress you up all over your bodies. Then there seemed to be the horticultural theme which linked *La Isla Bonita* (where lived young girls with eyes like potatoes) and *Express Yourself* (wherein Marilyn advised her sisters not to settle for eighteen carrots of gold.) But the fun reached its climax during *Into the Groove* when a spiteful and somewhat reckless Marilyn invited the animal-haters in the audience to step on the bee. Gary spluttered beer all over his suit.

'You like, eh?' A greasy piece in a CND T-shirt sidled up to him.

'Fantastic.'

'You want to meet Marilyn? Buy her drink?'

'Sure.' Gary pulled out his press pass. 'I'll throw in an interview, too.'

Mr CND stood back and looked at Gary with real respect. 'You are BBC?'

Gary nodded enthusiastically. This was more like it.

'Please.' Mr CND laid a hand reverently on Gary's arm, all but leaving grease spots. 'You will wait here – I go, I come, I take. Marilyn will be shocked with honour when I tell her. She very, very shy, must prepare self for interview mode.'

Gary nodded again. He could get used to this.

As he nodded, the shy performer on the rickety stage grabbed the crotch of her glittering leotard and yowled agonisingly. As she took her hand away, Gary saw a rainbow of sequins arc away from her crock of gold.

'That's a crock of shit,' said Marilyn wearily. She tapped her cigarette into her gin, did a double take and drank it anyway. Whatever she wasn't in the talent stakes, she was certainly a trooper.

Up close, surprisingly, she looked younger than she did onstage, despite the thick Kabuki-ish mask of make-up. He could see that she was still trying to look older than she was, which meant she was

261

young. When a woman tried to look younger than she was, she was finally old.

'No,' he lied, 'I really liked your act.'

'I don't think so.' She sighed and twisted to face herself in the dressing-table mirror. 'Listen, as you're not planning to write anything about me I'm going to take off my make-up. OK?'

'OK.'

She was very relaxed, so very soon after the show. He knew she was drinking – but he also sensed she was a junkie. Those long gloves covered more than baby fat.

'So what do you really want?' She twirled round to face him and let her puce negligée slip from a dimply shoulder. 'A date?'

'How about a chat?'

'Whatever you want to call it, big boy.' She twirled back to the mirror and began to peel off her thick false eyelashes. 'So long as you feed me first. But I warn you. I've got a very sweet tooth.'

Gary had been hoping to steer her towards the Green Frog on U radnice. The restaurant was a sinister vault whose very walls seemed body positive with grisly history red in tooth and claw. Prague's chief executioner had eaten there in the seventeenth century; Mydlar the Axeman, the black hooded hero who did his dance of death nightly through the deep blue dreams of the city's children. Ten of Mydlar's heads were piked and suspended over the Old Town Bridge for a whole decade only to be righteously buried in the Týn Church when the Protestant Saxons occupied Prague in 1631. Still the headless ones were said to haunt the bridge looking for the rest of them on every anniversary of their deaths, so obviously no-one had seen fit to break the news to them.

Apart from this, the food at the Green Frog was moderately cheap, and they did a great rare roast beef with garlic toast.

But it was closed. 'Never mind,' said Marilyn, pleased. 'Moskva's open till one ay em. We'll go there.' She took his arm and they made their way to the Russian restaurant on Na příkopě.

With each step, Gary groaned inwardly. Moskva was like a Russian fast-food joint which for some reason specialised in caviare, lobster and incredibly rich desserts. They accepted American

Express, but an arm and a leg would do just as nicely.

Marilyn perched on a high stool and ordered trifle, gateau and cheesecake, which she ate simultaneously with a fork while smiling sleepy-eyed across at Gary. When every dessert was finished she ordered a glass of brandy. Gary smiled back at her in a sickly way, thinking about his wallet.

'So. Mr Journalist.' She yawned and ran her finger around the rim of her glass. Quite a good rimmer, so far as he could judge. 'What do you really want?'

'Some information on a mutual friend.'

She raised a plucked eyebrow.

'Who?'

'Gustav.'

'You knew Gustav?'

'Yeah.' He held her gaze. 'He used to help me out sometimes. Do you know what I mean?'

She nodded agreeably. 'I've got a new man now. So if you ever need any stuff ... '

'I'm off for a few months.' He sniffed, hoping to look like an erstwhile junkie. 'A bit of clean living makes the kick all the more bigger when you get back on, don't you find?'

She smiled cynically; she looked prettier when she looked cynical, which was something he'd noticed about quite a lot of girls. 'I don't know. I've never been off it long enough to find out.'

'It was a bastard about Gustav, wasn't it?'

She nodded.

'A great guy like that.'

She nodded again. Was it the junkie nod, or did she genuinely not consider Gustav worth wasting words on?

'So young and all.'

She snorted. 'He was thirty-three, man! He said he was twenty-nine – no way!'

'Still.' Gary realised it was no good trying to play on her broken heart. Like all junkies, love was something reserved for the needle and the spoon, not the moon and June of romance. She had a new dealer now, and Gustav was dead. There was no gap in her life at all so long as the hole in her arm was filled. This was the one good thing about heroin, which otherwise he'd never been able to fathom.

She was looking around the restaurant, as openly curious as a child. He was losing her.

'I couldn't make it to the funeral,' he barged

on, 'but his old lady was inconsolable, someone told me. He was her only child, after all ... ' Maria's brief phone call had come in v. handy when it came to fleshing out the old human interest angle, he registered.

She shrugged. 'I didn't go either. That old bitch never liked me, and that place gives me the creeps.'

'Pardubice?'

'Semtex City. Whatever.' She put a cigarette between her lips and he lit it. 'You been there?'

'Just the once to see Gustav. It gave me the heebie jeebies.'

She laughed. 'Heebie jeebies. I like that.' She signalled to the waiter and pointed at her brandy glass, before holding up two fingers. Fuck, a double! How much more of this could his wallet take? Then she looked him straight in the eye like a junkie gunslinger, beaten but not yet down. 'So. What do you really want to know? Before I get too out of it to tell you anything at all.'

Gary leaned closer to her. 'I want to know how he died.'

She exhaled. In his face. It seemed to be unintentional, but you could never tell with women.

'He blew himself up in that car of his. Probably nodded out and a cigarette hit some petrol.'

'No, he didn't blow himself up. Semtex doesn't ignite unless it's detonated. And it certainly can't be detonated by a glowing fag butt.'

She made her eyes wide. 'Gustav didn't sell Semtex. He sold love. Love in little gram envelopes.'

'Gustav stopped selling smack three years ago when Semtex became a better bet, and you know it. We all know it. The newspapers called him an illegal arms dealer. The mystery isn't how he died, but who did it. Do you know?'

She pouted. 'If I tell you, what's in it for me?'

God, here it came; the Prague Chorus. What's in it for me — a gram of coke, a ticket to ride, a green card, a château in Washington DC, a life?

'A hundred American dollars,' he offered briskly.

'Get the fuck out of here!' She looked around and lowered her voice. 'Listen, I have a career. I make money good.' She leaned across the table; he could smell her scent, Poison. He'd never liked Poison; it smelled like old women's drawers. Maria used Arpège; it smelled like old money and new beginnings, she had once said. He wrenched his mind away from Maria and concentrated on Marilyn.

'I want to play some dates in London,' she announced. 'Not in America – I realise I'm not ready yet'. Yet! 'But in London you have the – lookalikes? And they do shows, yes?'

'That's right.' Was it? Gary tackled his memory for data on the London lookalike racket. 'There's a girl called Sara Lee, I think ... she plays nightclubs singing Madonna songs. And she's always in newspapers and on the TV modelling Madonna's old corsets – '

' – basques – '

' – basques. Whenever they're flogging them for some charity auction.'

'Does this Sara Lee look like Her?' Marilyn demanded.

'No, she's a lot better – ' Marilyn was flaring at him, well aware of her acute resemblance to her idol. 'I mean, she's got far less character,' he swerved smoothly.

'I bet she makes a lot more money than me, even,' Marilyn muttered. Then her face brightened; she was a bright sort of girl, he decided, which was very unusual for a junkie. 'And the smack in London – is it true that your country gives it free, through the doctor service?'

'Ah – yes.' Gary still found it rather unsettling that whenever he met a young European, the main thing they were interested in about his island home was the myth of the junkie Eldorado where the morning dose was not just grudgingly decriminalised but actually forced free and gratis on the deserving junkie like some daily Welcome Wagon gift.

'Yes, I want to come to London,' Marilyn decided. 'Not to immigrate – you don't have to fiddle me any papers or that sort of hassle. I'll get a work permit for a few months – all you have to do is make sure I have a good hotel, lots of press exposure etcetera. If I meet someone I like, I may get married. It all depends.'

He looked at her with mild admiration. It was strange to think that a none-too-attractive junkie girl seemed to have a lot more pride, motivation and self-regard than Maria, who seemed so fierce, fit and clever.

'I think we can manage that,' he said. They probably could; if not he and the World Service then he and Marco, or he and Max, or even he and Nikki and her sleazy PR man if he played his cards right. It wasn't too difficult to get an exhibitionistic girl publicity in London these days; with the Madonna angle, and the Czech twist, it would be easier for Marilyn than most.

'Good' She looked around, seized a paper napkin and took a pen from her bag. 'Right – "I – "' What's your name?'

'Gary First. But – '

' "I, Gary First, promise that I will aid Mariana Zoubek – " that's my real name – "in hotel and publicity purposes during her forthcoming tour of London, England. Though not available to escort her in person, I will en-en – "' She looked at him questioningly.

'Endeavour.'

' " – to meet her requirements by proxy."' She pushed the napkin and pen towards him.

'Sign and date, please.'

Cursing himself silently, he did what she told him.

'That's more like it' She glanced at the napkin and secreted it in her bag. 'So. Ask away.'

Now the moment had finally come, he had

forgotten what he was going to ask. A simple one for starters. 'Do you know the names of the people Gustav was doing business with in the weeks before he died?'

'Yes' Mariana was routing through her bag again. 'I'm just going to the toilets for a celebration shot. I'll only be a minute.'

One minute. Two minutes. Three, four, five. Ten minutes. Gary got to his feet, asked a waiter and found the Ladies.

He listened for a minute by the outer door, then pushed it open very slightly. 'Marilyn?' There was no answer. 'Mariana?'

He walked into the room. Only one cubicle showed a closed door. From behind it, utter silence. He tapped on it. 'Mariana?'

There was no answer.

They'd got her; the bastards had got her. Must have followed them here from the Cashbox and moved in when she came for her shot. Probably they'd simply shot her up with an overdose of her own stash, so it would look like yet another wretched lavatory OD.

He began to rattle the door, then to kick it.

He was just about to go out into the dining

room and break the news to the management when a bolt shot back and Mariana staggered out. 'What's all the noise?'

'I thought you were dead.' He gaped at her.

'Sorry. I nodded out. I feel fine now.' She offered her arm with a funny old-fashioned gesture. 'Shall we?'

They walked back to their table; anxious waiters swooped on them, relieved that they hadn't done a runner. 'For me, another brandy. Double,' said Mariana. 'And for the gentleman too.'

This time he accepted it, for his nerves. They were settled with their drinks when Mariana spoke. 'OK. Names of people he dealt with. Well, there were so many. Why don't you tell me the one you're looking for, and I can tell you if I've heard of him.'

He sipped his brandy. But that way, he realised, she could simply say yes or no to any name. He had to get her to do some work in order to establish her credentials.

'I'll give you an initial. J.'

'Jiri?'

'No.'

'Jasper?'

'No'

'Jan?'

'For Pete's sake!'

'But Pete doesn't begin with a J!'

'This is just stupid. It's like Twenty bloody Questions. Animal, vegetable or mineral?'

'What is mineral?' She blinked at him.

You are, you dumb cluck! he wanted to yell. But it wasn't fair on the poor broad; she was junked to the gills, drunk up to the eyeballs, recovering from a hectic evening of stepping on bees and generally the worse for wear. He'd have to try another tack. 'Look.' He took her hands between his and stared urgently into her face. She was fading fast. 'Did Gustav ever sell to an American?'

'Oh, sure. You mean Mr LaMonte at the Embassy?' She leaned across the table and her eyes gleamed. Conspiracy theorists were the same the world over; it was, like sex, an international language. 'He was CIA, Gustav said!'

'That's right.' His mouth was dry.

'Right! But then ... ' Her voice trailed off.

'What?'

'Gustav said so many things when he was stoned. Sometimes he said he was a double agent

– working for the Americans and the Soviets. If the blow was especially good, he'd claim to be a triple agent – the Americans, Russians and Libyans. It was a joke among our friends that you could test the strength of dope by giving a toke to Gustav and hearing how many people he thought he was working for *that* night.'

'Oh.' A dopehead. Even more of an unreliable witness than a bloke who was convinced he'd come into being on a potter's wheel.

'And, of course, towards the end he was boasting more than ever … '

'Towards the end of what?'

Mariana sighed and looked down into her brandy. 'I'm not a bitch, ya know? But I was getting pissed off. I wanted to tour abroad, like I told you. I told Gustav that if he wouldn't help me, put some money into publicity and things, I would leave him. That's when he started overtime with the bragging. There was always going to be this one last deal and then everything would be peachy. Of course I'd heard it all a million times. But then he introduced me to this guy from the Embassy – Mr LaMonte. Told the guy I couldn't spikka da English. The guy swallowed it. Dumb fuck. I speak great English. I learned it from Duran Duran records. My favourite is *Hungry Like a Wolf*. Mariana smiled mistily for her lost girlhood.

'What did he look like?' Gary urged her.

'A tall guy, thin, very fair. Should have been handsome but he wasn't, somehow. Gave me the creeps. Just like you imagine CIA guys to be. Though Gustav said he was some rich bigshot who just did it for kicks. Gustav thought that made him better. But I thought it made him worse.'

Gary nodded.

'So then everything was great for a while. Mr LaMonte was the big one he'd been waiting for. But then something happened; they fought, I think. Shouting, there was. After that Gustav wasn't so keen on the idea.'

'Did he tell you why?'

She shook her head. 'No, but he got very paranoid. I wasn't really that interested in that side of his life – I'm more the creative type – and he wasn't desperate to talk to anyone about it. There was the usual stuff when he was drunk – the Russians, the American, the Libyans. And the CIA.

You name it.' She shrugged. 'So one day he goes out – and he don't come back.'

He looked at her seriously. 'Is that all you know?'

'Yes.' She smiled. 'Do you want to come back for coffee?'

Mariana lived across the Vltava in Smíchov; a few minutes from the centre of Prague, but a world away, it seemed to Gary. In the nineteenth century it had become the capital's industrial centre and brewery, and living there was still a dirty job – but lots of people seemed to like doing it. The raw urban roar of the heavy traffic and powerhouse factories were leavened by the presence of Prague's gypsies, until on summer evenings the district sometimes seemed like a more tranquil version of blue-collar Manhattan. Teenagers cursed each other from tenement windows, gangs kicked their heels on street corners and music blared from apartments. Gary half expected to see the Jets and the Sharks come swinging down the street as he followed Mariana past the Malá Strana Cemetery.

'What is that place?' It was corny, but he couldn't help shivering.

'It was opened during the plague in the seventeenth-century. To pick up the extra trade.' She lurched against him. 'It's been out of use for a hundred years. That's why it's like a huge sea of ivy. Those bumps and lumps are the tombs and headstones beneath. The huge lump in the middle is where one of our most famous bishops is buried. In a cast-iron tomb.'

'Was he bigger than Madonna?' He couldn't help smiling. He had grown a little fond of Mariana-Marilyn in the long evening since he had first seen her grab her crotch and yowl.

'You bet.'

They stopped and stared into the huge, eerie cemetery, the consuming ivy cushioning decapitated stone angels and smashed crucifixes. Huge yawning tombs bore witness to the fact that this cemetery was, for reasons superstitious or economic (and probably both, knowing the Czechs), being allowed to crumble away into nothingness.

'Madonna would love this place,' said Gary. 'All those crosses. All this decay. I can just see her making a video here.'

'Yeah. She can come here, and I'll move into her place in Malibu.' Mariana giggled. 'Come on.'

The flat was large, especially for an Eastern bloc capital, both strangely bare and cluttered, and none too clean. Posters calling the unwashed faithful to long-gone Western pop concerts decorated (if that was the word) the off-white (or on-grey, to be brutally frank) walls of the big living room. Here, in opposing corners, there were two shrines; one to Western technology, in the shape of the big television, video recorder and stereo/CD system and the other to Madonna. Nightlights guttered petulantly around posters, eight by ten glossies and dying flowers. In every dream home a heartache, and here was Mariana's.

Gary checked the Japanese labels on the hardware; Gustav had been making serious money, no doubt about it.

'Drink?' called Mariana. She had collapsed on to the on-grey sofa and was holding up a bottle of Malibu like a white flag, surrendering to the forces of drunkenness. Malibu, for frigaboo's sake – as if the Czechs didn't have enough problems!

'Got any beer?'

'Sure.' Smashed though she was, she got up and staggered out, presumably to the kitchen. 'Just be a minute.'

He looked around the room furtively. It was a mess. But had it been burgled by LaMonte's geeks looking for something incriminating, or was Mariana simply a lousy housekeeper, like most junkie brides?

Here she was, clutching his open beer, barely able to walk without the support of the wall. Gary looked at her calculatingly. His head suddenly felt very clear. 'Nice place you've got.'

'Yeah. Sorry it's such a mess. It's real hard to get a good maid in Prague' She fell on to the sofa. 'OOOF!'

'That's a piece of Czech I undertstood' He came to the sofa and smiled down at her, accepting his beer.

'What was?' She grinned woozily.

'OOOF! It meant, roughly translated, "My feet are killing me." It's pretty much the same in English, too.'

'My feet, and my corset.' She sprawled there, smiling up at him.

'Here.' He bent down and swung her legs round

on to the sofa. Then he poured her a double measure of Malibu into a smeary glass. 'Say when.'

'Never.'

They laughed.

'Do you want juice in it?'

'No, I like the taste. Cheers.' Most of the Malibu went over Mariana, but about a third hit the target.

She looked at him curiously over the rim of her glass, then put it unsteadily down on the on-grey carpet. She snuggled luxuriously down into the sofa and yawned. 'There's a coat there. On that chair. Tuck me up, please. I'm very cold.'

He put the coat over her. It whiffed to high heaven. A smelly hippie greatcoat. It must have been Gustav's.

'You don't want to fuck me, do you?' She said sleepily, smiling secretly to herself.

'No.'

'Good.' She stretched and spoke quietly, confidentially and almost soberly. 'I hate sex.' Within half a minute she was asleep and snoring gently. Her snore was melodic, rhythmic and easy on the ear. It was, actually, much better than her singing voice.

Gary looked down at her. Relaxed, with the make-up mask evaporated and the blind blonde ambition dormant, she was childishly pretty.

'Goodnight, sleeping beauty,' he said softly, and turned away.

Right. The rest of the flat first. Give her time to settle before you take this room to pieces. He walked through the dark and grimy maroon passageway to the furthest point from the living room. The kitchen; big white Western fridge and cooker, thick with grease. Unwashed mugs, most of which proclaimed I HEART NEW YORK. Nothing in the fridge but a bearded sausage, a wizened lemon and three splits of bad champagne. A hooker's fridge, bless her.

There was a cupboard. Its bareness screamed its innocence. In the other cupboard under the sink he found a spectacular amount of mildew, a sparkling collection of detergents which the proud owners had obviously found too attractive to sully by using, and a long dead lump of hash wedged under a black plastic bucket.

Gary straightened up, holding the item between forefinger and thumb. He looked at it in disgust, more at himself than the dead doper. Hot going, boy wonder! Get any sharper than this and you'll get a Boy Scout badge for Nature Study!

He tried the bathroom; Lord have mercy, here was the Tennis Girl Scratching BTM poster! Right opposite the john, too. The thought of a contemplative and constipated Gustav pulling his rancid salami before it each morning was not a nice one. Gary made a perfunctory search of the medicine cabinet and got out. Lots of suppositories and cough mixture – the answer to a junkie's prayer.

The bedroom was, sadly, just the sort of bedroom you'd imagine an arms-dealing doper and a heroin-addicted nightclub singer would have chosen in which to sanctify their love. It was red, like a huge womb which was a lifelong stranger to spring cleaning. A water bed sloshed incontinently, which must have made Gustav well jealous. Clothes lay everywhere, past complaining, seduced and abandoned by a girl in a hurry. And the whole set up stank worse than Gustav's greatcoat. Was the guy still here or something?

Gary automatically crossed the room to wrench open a window. He stopped himself, cursing. You stupid fuck, you'll make someone a lovely wife one day. Especially when Johnson's had your balls for breakfast. Stop it. You're not here to play house. You're here to kick butt. CIA butt.

He walked back into the living room. Mariana shifted sulkily on the sofa. 'A million dollars,' she mumbled. Even asleep she aimed high.

He approached her and knelt down. Let's see; wine with dinner, brandy after. Malibu. Lashings of heroin. How out was she? Gingerly he tugged at Gustav's coat.

She grabbed it back fiercely.

Careful. She's a junkie. She gets colder than most people. He leaned over and felt the radiator. Stone cold. Too bad. No time to fuck with thermostats now. The heat was on.

He relinquished the coat. After a few seconds the snore started up. Now he began to pat the coat, but gently. Little baby pats, all over.

His hand touched metal.

It slipped into the funky pocket and closed around keys.

It pulled them out carefully, stifling their tell-tale jangle.

Three doorkeys – to here, his mother's place in Semtex City and to some sort of warehouse, probably.

And one smaller key. To a desk, or a strongbox.

He stood up and looked around the room. There was nothing it could have fitted. He sighed and looked down at the sleeping girl. Best to take the keys and leave her to her dreams. Maybe he could try Gustav's mother next. Yeah, sure; take her out, feed her lobster and Malibu, get her smashed. Should be easy in a swinging city like Pardubice. God, he despised himself. He was one step removed from Tomas; a loony with a lame-brained crusade.

Behind him, in the corner, a spray of dead blossom fell into one of the shrine's nightlights. Flame flared.

He ran to it, and blew on it. It only spread. He grabbed the long front drape of the heavy red velvet tablecloth the shrine reposed upon, and successfully stifled the small fire with it.

Where the long drape had been, exposed metal glinted at him.

Hi there, big boy, it seemed to say. We've had a date for a long time now. And better late than never.

Slowly, quietly, almost respectfully, he began to dismantle Mariana's shrine to Madonna.

15

Officer Hus gazed across the desk at Gary First, more in sorrow than in anger.

'It's you. It's really you, isn't it, Mr First? When my man told me you were back, I didn't want to believe it. I said, No, Jan. It's just someone who looks like Mr First. With the same name, maybe. But it is absolutely not *my* Mr First. Not the one who played the horrible trick with the Creature on me, after wasting my time and gaining my trust. It was cruel the first time, I said to my man Jan. But no-one would be so cruel as to humiliate the same victim twice.'

Gary made an involuntary hand-wringing movement. Policemen always made him nervous. But Hus was so decent, so disgusted, so ... Gene Hackman. It was more than he could bear to have Gene Hackman look at him in that decent, disgusted way.

'Officer Hus, I beg of you ... '

Hus sighed. 'OK. What is it now? Frankenstein's lost his bride? Dracula's mother has gone missing? Or perhaps the Mummy has lost his Daddy. Please tell me now and put me out of my suspension.'

'It's worse.' Gary gulped, swinging the suitcase up on to the desk and popping its locks. 'It's this.'

Any other man would have drawn back, or at least shown surprise. But Hus just raised an eyebrow, and peered into the case like a housewife inspecting a new brand of brush. He took in the the three blocks of Semtex and the bundles of hundred-dollar bills. He took in the guns and the five cassette tapes. He pointed at them and then looked at Gary. He looked only mildly curious.

'What's on them?'

'It's the man who was blown up in the forest near Pardubice last month. He'd been dealing Semtex to foreigners, illegally. Then he caught a big one – LaMonte Johnson from the US Embassy. Pawel – that's his name, Gustav Pawel – didn't trust him. So I guess these tapes were his insurance. That and a sort of Living Will.'

'Put one on there.' Hus gestured at a hefty tape machine to one side of his desk.

Gary did so. Soon Gustav's stoned babble filled the room. He had a strong American accent, like all Czechs who took drugs.

'Hi, Mariana. Hi, my lady. This is for you, OK? Just to say I love you. And if you're receiving me … deceiving me … '

'What is it he is on?' demanded Hus of Gary, as if he had been the Groover's man. He shrugged.

' … then I'm gone to the great free gig in the sky. And I want to lay it on you who sent me here … an eye for an eye. Turn, turn, turn.'

Hus and Gary made eye contact, briefly and beautifully on the same wavelength. They were thinking what a monumental wanker old Groovy Gustav had been.

'You remember that guy from the Embassy? The one you never dug? I got in deep shit with him, man. Promised him more than I had. Then I see I didn't have it. He said I was holding out on him. That's when I got weird.' Gustav chuckled nostalgically. 'Remember that time I caught you holding out on me with the stash? And I bust your lip?'

'Happy days,' said Gary wryly.

'Happy days,' sighed Gustav sincerely. 'Anyway ... the dude didn't believe me, I guess. Thought I was two-timing him with the Libyans. Because here I am. DOA. It's funny, being dead. It's not much different from being alive.' There was a pause; the confusion behind it almost audible. 'Wait. Hey, I *am* still alive!'

'Why's he talking in English, do you think?'

'Because it's a performance.' Hus lit a cigarette without offering Gary one, totally absorbed. 'Our young people, when they perform they do it English. They think our language don't give them too much to be that proud about – '

'Robot and pistol – '

' – and Semtex. Yeah, great. Also it's American, English. They like the American way ... '

'So listen,' the dead man interrupted them impatiently, 'it's Milos. Milos helped them get me. My best buddy! And he'll do the deal, with the extra he got. He was holding out on me, too. He'll do it the usual place ... ah, you know where. It would be at six pee em, on the last Friday of – '

Hus and Gary looked at each other, tense and somehow shy.

' – this month,' Gustav flourished lamely.

'What month?'

Hus shook his head, reassuring. 'We'll try it' Then he nodded at Gary, as though he was one of his men. As though he had done a good job.

'You can go to the fuzz. Whatever.' Gustav gave it the big finish. 'But just so you know the bottom line, babe, I got one more thing to say – '

Hus and Gary looked at each other like lovers caught in adultery, both proud and full of fear for what came next. They literally caught their breath.

'Sex. And drugs. And rock and roll.'

The tape clicked off.

Hus rolled his eyes. He offered Gary a cigarette, finally. 'Excuse.' He hit the tape machine and took out the tape, nursing it in his hand. 'These people. Selling the Semtex. They don't think about their country. Out it goes, kills people. And to the West, it's still Czechs doing it. They're traitors, these people, of the worst sort. Ten years ago, we would have shot them.' He smiled a sad Communist smile. 'Americans, eh? I can use an American.' He shot a gorgeous grin at Gary and made a slicing movement across his shining head; from ear to shining ear. 'Scalp 'em. Like the Indians did.'

Gary grinned. It was OK. Hus liked him, at last.

'Who is this Mariana?'

'A singer. I met her. She's really nice.' He was aware how defensive he sounded.

'Sure, sure.' Hus grinned. 'A singer, yeah?' He put out his cigarette, moving impatiently now. 'Yeah, she'll sing!' He reached for the phone.

Gary perched on the desk. At last he felt at ease with his hero. He smiled lovingly. 'You've seen a lot of American cop movies, I bet.'

'You bet' Hus was dialling now, reaching out across the city to cinch a certain number, but he had the time and the grace to give Gary his good side, posing. 'Don't say it. I look just like Gene Hackman, no?'

'What are we waiting for?' Gary hissed at Hus.

'Mr First, do us all a favour and shut the fock up, OK?' Huss hissed back at him. Try saying *that* when you've had a few.

The two of them and three of Hus's men sat closer than nature intended in the back of a van not far from the hotel, trying to hear what the men in Suite 101 were saying. They were speaking in English but might as well not have been as far as Gary was concerned; for every one word he could make out, ten were a mess of squeaks and crackle. He sighed and sat back, imagining the glory that would soon be his, to pass the time.

The big treatment by the World Service, syndication in the world's newspapers – fuck it, he'd be bigger than Woodward and Bernstein put together. Then of course he'd get the offer to write the book – might even have to have one of those auction things, they sounded good – and there could easily be a film. Clive Owen could play him. And last but not least, there was the money; serious money, the sort even *she* would respect.

He grinned around at the four Czechs. 'OK, guys?'

They said nothing, and Gary suddenly sensed

that beneath their stoic silence lay fear. His dream was their danger. They had the weapon of surprise, but the men they would be dealing with were armed and, when cornered, probably dangerous. One wrong move, a bit of bad luck and someone could easily get his face blown away.

For the first time Gary wondered whether he should take Hus's advice and stay in the van.

Inside Suite 101, LaMonte Johnson sat scrutinising Milos as he bent his head over his work. Milos was a small, skinny guy with big brown eyes and a mouth that never stopped; this much was clear. LaMonte considered himself a shrewd judge of character; he could spot an asshole, a bullshitter, a clown or a cretin at eight paces. But Milos had him baffled. Which one was he?

As a diplomat of some experience, LaMonte knew how to make small talk in all the major languages. However, the idiom Milos seemed partial to was something new and rather puzzling.

'Yo, my main man Monty! What, it isn't?' Milos had exclaimed and then queried on entering the suite. He had a big suitcase and a brace of even bigger bodyguards.

LaMonte had smiled and stuck out a hand, which Milos promptly slapped. This seemed to tickle the Czech something rotten. 'So square, man!' he wheezed to his large associates, who sniggered like psychotic schoolgirls.

LaMonte was about to introduce his aide when Milos charged up to Stacey Charms, a big black man in a blue blazer.

'Dig those shoes, man – they FBI-CIA shoes! I can cop you cats straightaways. How you do, homeboy?'

Milos raised his fist to exchange fraternal greetings, the way he'd seen American blacks do in all his favourite movies.

'Bitching, cuz, jus' bitching,' answered Charms smoothly. He executed a brother's handshake so complex and cool that even Johnson was impressed.

'I love this dude!' husked Milos.

In meetings like this, LaMonte knew, it was necessary to take control, establish the topics of conversation, the rhythm and mood of the participants. But how could he take control of a wack like Milos, who was totally out of control? He tried to steer the conversation straight on to the Semtex ban, but Milos wanted to know about Paula Abdul, MTV and most of all Eddie Murphy. He embarked on a medley of scenes from his favourite Murphy films and soon the strain of smiling raptly was telling on LaMonte. God knows, he'd suffered incessant performances of native dancing and national folk songs in the hallowed name of diplomacy, but this took the bloody cake. Milos was either the biggest asshole or the best actor he'd ever met; whatever, he was going to have to muster all the diplomatic skills he possessed to prevent himself from throttling the moron.

'Life is weird, uh? Here I am sitting in a flash suite with CIA. Chillin'! Me! Ha! If my old lady could see me now! She was a good Communist, God rest her soul; turned in my father, he went to prison and died there. Now there was a woman of principle! Eh?'

LaMonte smiled. He looked at the suitcase. 'Perhaps we should get down to business … '

'Business, yay.' Milos snapped his fingers. 'Yo, homeboy, bring that bag over here.'

One of the goons brought the case to the table. Milos began to tackle the combination lock. 'Hope I get it right, man. One wrong digit and boom, we all going up to heaven! That would be funny, eh, Monty?'

'Hilarious,' said Johnson. 'Apart from the fact that this stuff is the most stable explosive the world has ever seen.'

'You too sharp for me, my man! But that don't explain what happened to my main man Gus, eh?' Milos looked at him with crafty eyes. 'Come and get a load of this.'

LaMonte walked round the case and stared in at the tightly packed blocks wrapped in waxy orange paper. He nodded, and looked over at Stacey Charms, inclining his head. The aide picked up a shiny briefcase and set it down next to the suitcase.

Milos picked it up without looking into it.

'You're not going to check?'

'Why would I do a thing like that?' Milos twinkled horribly. 'I got what you need, homeboy. Everybody gonna get well!'

'Right. Well ... ' Johnson looked at Charms, who shrugged. 'I think you and your men should leave first.'

'Sure thing.' Hefting the case in his hand, Milos stood by the door, grinning. 'We get together sometime soon and hang loose, say wha? Maybe in the States.'

'That would be delightful,' LaMonte heard himself say.

Milos opened the door and stepped into a gun barrel. As he thought better of leaving so soon, three armed policemen burst in.

'Shit!' said Charms.

Milos' bodyguards threw themselves on to the floor, begging in Czech not be shot. Milos went up to them and began to put the boot in with intent; first one great ape, then the other got the benefit of his Air Jordans in their huge ribs.

LaMonte Johnson sat down on the sofa and began to adjust his tie.

Suddenly, into all this marched the slight figure of Gary First, Officer Hus behind him. Gary strode up to Johnson, shoved a finger under his chin and said in his best *Sweeney* voice, 'You're nicked, sunshine.'

Gary was tossed into the cell like a guest's overcoat being thrown on a party bed.

You have to laugh, he thought, wiping away the

tears and sweat that coursed down his face.

He'd been interrogated for four hours – make it five, including the waiting between bouts. Fucking *Midnight Express* all over again, he thought; by which he meant one short slap around the face for being cheeky. Then there was the kick in the nuts his own Officer Hus had given him in Suite 101. That had hurt most of all.

What would happen to him now? There were still lots of nutters in the VB. They might torture him. Hadn't they yelled at him that he was a British spy? But then they'd also accused him of being a drug dealer, an arms dealer and something called an 'English woofter.' In fact, they'd called him just about everything except what he really was; a fucking buffoon, with knobs on.

Two uniformed men entered the cell suddenly; two men he hadn't seen before. Nasty bastards with little eyes close together. Were they the heavy mob? He was for it.

'Come with us, please, Mr First,' said one of them grimly.

Gary shook his head, attempting to cower against the cell wall with some measure of dignity. 'I demand to see a lawyer.'

'Mr First, please – '

'You won't get away with this! I warn you! I want to call my Embassy.'

With no more ado the men grabbed Gary by the arms and dragged him from the cell.

'You bastards!' he screamed, kicking out like Milos in a moody. 'I'm British, you bastards! We fought the Second World War for you! You'd be saluting the swastika now if it wasn't for me ... please! Let me go! I'll do anything you say!'

They threw him into a room; cold and bare, and probably the scene of many a forced confession. The door slammed and he lay on the floor for a few seconds, weeping.

Then he saw a pair of shiny black shoes.

He grabbed them, then a pair of grey flannel trousers. Then he buried his face in a pair of scrawny but oddly reassuring knees. 'Please!' he squealed. 'Don't hurt me! I beg of you!'

'No-one is going to hurt you, Gary?'

He froze. Then he looked up.

It was LaMonte.

The American smiled. 'Come on. I'll take you home.'

In the back seat of his limousine, LaMonte handed Gary an immaculate linen handkerchief.

Gary took it without meeting his eyes. 'Thanks.' He blew his nose and then neatly folded the cloth before giving it back, still staring straight ahead.

'You keep it,' said LaMonte gently, turning back the hand which sought to press this sopping offering on him. He leaned over to the car bar and poured a large brandy. 'Here. Drink this. You'll soon feel better.'

'Nothing will ever make me feel better.' Gary gulped. 'But thanks.'

There was a silence.

'And sorry.'

'For what?'

You had to hand it to the guy, Gary thought, he had class. No gloating, just an open-handed and open-hearted generosity. He'd always wondered what she saw in him – it had to be more than money – and now he knew. The hard way.

'Sorry for fucking everything up for you. But I thought you were … ' He was aware of how whiney he sounded, and what a contrast there was between them. It was the crucial, crushing difference between being a boy and being a man.

'You thought I was up to something dirty. You heard the word – letters, rather – CIA, and you assumed it was something nasty I was working on here. Yeah, we certainly seem to have something of an image problem abroad.' Johnson laughed broodingly. There was a silence while they both thought about what had almost happened, and what had happened instead.

'What I don't understand is why you had – I mean, shouldn't the Czech police be dealing with this sort of thing? Or the Czech, I don't know, secret services?'

'Of course they should – but they can't be trusted to. Too many of them are left over from the old set-up. They're not going to cut off their Semtex to spite their salaries. So the Government had to ask a foreign bureau to do it.'

'But why the CI – I mean, why you guys?'

'Because we want to stop this stuff from getting into the Middle East more than anyone else. We can't risk another Lockerbie. When the citizens of any country get killed, that country hurts. But America does more than hurt. It feels completely and totally castrated. The whole world isn't just feeling sorry for us; in some secret way, it feels glad we're hurting, too.'

'And now I've blown it all for you.' Gary put his face in his hands. 'I'm so sorry.'

'Well, this particular operation is blown, as you say.' LaMonte sighed. 'But the battle goes on. And in the end, we'll get them.'

'Did you kill Gustav? Or was it Milos?'

LaMonte looked at him sideways. 'The less you know, the better. Even now, Ah, here we are.'

The car had pulled up outside his apartment building. Gary turned to LaMonte, his hand on the door. 'Why have you been so good to me? It's hardly in the national interest – or yours either, come to that.'

LaMonte laughed and shook his head. 'Gary, Gary ... I could give you a hundred reasons, none of which you'd believe. Let's just say that, despite all appearances, I'm a real nice guy. And you – you're young and dumb, but your heart's in the right place. Even when your brain goes AWOL. You did wrong, but you did it for all the right reasons.'

He was too tired to lie. Better to just get out of the car, up the stairs and into bed, where he could probably stay for the rest of his life now without anybody missing him.

'Well, Mr Johnson, thanks. Knowing you has been an education, and probably the only useful one I've ever had. Good night – and God bless America.'

'Goodbye, Gary.'

He stood alone on the sidewalk, watching the man in the long black limousine disappear from his life.

16

So it was all over. His big story, his big dream. Gary took stock of his brilliant career and found that the cupboard was all but bare.

All that was left seemed to be the Lost Girls. And who could he turn to for one last chance but *the* Lost Girl?

Gary looked at the tacky taupe Trimfone in his flat on Malá Strana and marvelled at the fact that it was only seven weeks since he'd used the telephonic mode to break off his – no, *not* relationship; *physical friendship* with Nikki.

That he could ever have the telephonic upper hand over anyone again, man, woman, child or heavy breather, struck him as the height of improbability. The telephone was like a high-tech attack dog; it seemed to smell your fear and magnify it to max quad proportions. Every tremor and quaver was picked up and highlighted and poured into the ear of the receiver like a liquid gold gift. Once shattered, phonic phoney confidence was impossible to fake.

He dialled her number, dying by digits. It was ringing – once, twice, three times. Was there a dialling tone in Hell? 'Hello?' There was a Hell in Hello, that much was certain.

'Maria?'

Her voice grew thorns. 'What do *you* want?'

'I've got to see you.'

'No thank you.' She gave something between a snort and a snigger. 'If I want to be humiliated, I'll sleep with my fiancé.'

'*Please.*' He swallowed. 'It's not about you, or me. Or my career. It's important.' He knew he was going to sound like a bit of *Casablanca* which had quite justifiably ended up on the cutting-room floor, but he couldn't think of any feasible alternative. 'It's about Czechoslovakia.'

She burst into a gale of rude laughter. 'What's your problem? Can't you get your preferred brand of mineral water? Is there an aftershave shortage? Something crucial like that?' She snarled, all humour blanched from the dry bones of her loathing. 'Can't you pester your Embassy about it? We're busy people. We're packing to leave.' She gave a real smoker's laugh, so sexy in this age of the pathology of pleasure. 'The Western way, no? Movin' on.'

'The G is not silent, Maria.' He couldn't help correcting her, the cow. 'Unless you're a Seventies Laurel Canyon rock star with more coke dealers than album credits.'

She hissed. Then laughed, with some effort. 'Goodbye, Gary!'

'*Please*.' Totally obdurate; the word had never sounded less like a plea. It was instead the soundbite syllable of a man getting his rubber-soled foot in the door, shameless. Well, he felt blameless; she was a combative woman, Maria Vachss, combative to the point of pure mania. This was the only way to match her; the only game in town to match the only dame in town. The only one worth having, anyhow.

Then her voice broke – but only slightly. 'What do you *want* from me, Gary?' It was the nearest she had ever come to pleading with him, it seemed. But now he was too driven to feel smug.

'Your help.' His voice was crisp, almost cruel. 'Tell a lie – your boyfriend's help.'

'What?' She laughed, disbelievingly. 'Isn't that a little strong, Gary? I mean, even from you?'

He decided to brazen it out. What you mean, white boy, *decided*? There was just no other way out. 'Why? I did him a favour, didn't I? Sent you right slap bang into his bed by being the man I am rather than the man you wanted me to be?' He was already tough, and now he got tougher. 'He's won. And he owes me one.'

She was silent. Then she laughed in silver amazement. 'Gary, you're incorrigible. But you're so like me! So I can't really hate you, can I? Because that would mean I hated myself. And that would be self-loathing, which is highly un-American, no?' She stopped, then spoke through a smile; he could tell. He'd won. Silently he did a lap of triumph around the Trimfone. 'When do you want to see him?'

In a heavily guarded mansion block near the US Embassy, LaMonte Johnson's apartment spoke the international language of interior design and decoration. American space combined with English comfort, dusted with a patina of old-style Middle European plushness.

Maria Vachss sat on one of the three red velvet sofas, huddled inside black leggings and a black cashmere sweater, her legs beneath her, drinking good champagne with a bad grace.

LaMonte Johnson smiled lovingly at her beautiful, sulky face, and then turned to gaze through his big-windowed wall down at the beautiful, sulky city, the sun setting red behind it. How he loved them both.

There was a knock on the door, and a young maid entered. LaMonte was well aware that the English, bless them, considered such coyness declassé. He didn't give a damn whether his staff knocked or not. But for some reason – be bold, be bold, but not *too* bold – they seemed to prefer to.

He smiled again, turning to the girl.

'Yes, Tereza?'

'Is Mr First, sir.' Tereza winked at him. It was a nervous tic, not an impudence, but it never failed to delight and amuse him.

'Why are you winking, idiot?' Maria snapped from the couch.

'For the same reason you are drinking, my darling,' came back LaMonte without missing a beat. 'Because the girl can't help it.' Maria gaped at him, and he went and took Tereza's hand. 'For my fiancée, I apologise. She is tense tonight. Already she misses her beautiful country.'

'I can apologise for myself, thank you, LaMonte. Even if I can't keep myself in the style to which you've so thoughtfully made me accustomed.' She held out her arms to Tereza. 'Tisha, come here and slap me. I'm such a bitch.'

Tereza shook her head, smiling slowly and winking profoundly. She adored Maria.

'Show him in, please, Tereza.' The girl left and LaMonte turned to Maria. She tossed back yet another glass of Bollinger, grimacing as though it were liver salts. He smiled coldly. 'Complaining about affluence, now, my darling, and you haven't even passed Ellis Island. What a neurotic little American girl you are, already.'

'Fuck you, asshole.'

'Spoken like a true Yankee slut.' He smiled again. 'Pull yourself together for a few moments, if you can.'

'Why don't you come and kiss me, so I can throw all this expensive shit up and get sober again?'

Gary caught them in mid-snarl as Tereza showed him in, winking at him meaningfully as she left. Maria and LaMonte looked sheepish and retreated as he walked in awkwardly, holding out his hand to Johnson.

'Mr Johnson. Thank you for agreeing to see me.'

'My pleasure.' Johnson signalled to two armchairs; he sat in one with his back to Maria, and gestured Gary into the other, facing her. 'And by the way, you stay on two unconditional conditions. One, that you call me LaMonte and two, that we call what happened history.'

Johnson swivelled, laughing smugly at Maria, who raised her bottle blearily. He turned back to Gary, chuckling indulgently. 'My fiancée, as you've no doubt gathered by now by her relentless determination not to acknowledge your presence, bears a grudge with all the fierceness of her for-bears – an ancient people, with long memories. And *great* mammaries.' He laughed again, then appeared to have a terrible attack of earnestness, leaning forward to Gary. 'That's how I know your trouble must be serious; she hates you, but she loves her people more.'

How little he knows her, Gary wondered.

'So what gives?'

Gary took a deep breath. 'I have reason to believe that there is a traffic in young women, from Czechoslovakia to the USA. They're promised good jobs and then they're made into whores. Hopeless junkie whores, that is – not the happy hookers of legend.' He stopped, his nerve running out. 'So I wondered if you'd heard anything about it.'

He looked up from his bitten nails to LaMonte's face. He gasped; the man looked Un-Dead – numb, dumbstruck and paler than it seemed possible for a human being to be without being declared officially deceased. He looked not at Gary but through him, with brimming, unfocused eyes, and when he spoke he was no longer the loud, self-satisfied American – but the most humbled, and the quietest American the world had ever seen. As Gary watched him, he buried that terrible face in those translucent, skeletal hands, the deep aquamarine veins on them standing out lividly like a junkie's wet dream. And when he looked up, he was UnDead no longer; just infinitely weary and determined.

'Yes – yes, I do know something about this – thing. This awful, awful thing.' He shook his head disbelievingly. 'In fact, I've known something about it for a long time. And by the time I leave here next week, I believe I'll know damn near everything. Where the cheques are cashed, where the bodies are buried – the whole sad, sick can of worms.'

From the couch, Maria hiccuped coarsely.

LaMonte forward, grasping Gary's hands in his. Once again Gary felt that strange, electric shocky feeling. But it didn't seem cricket to shove the poor guy away. 'Like you, Gary, I've come to love this country. I can't stand to think of it raped by the West – its people turning into the sort of human garbage you see back home on every street corner.

Do you *know* why I'm being sent back? – not because I want to go, I'd stay here forever. No – I'm being sent back because I know too much about this filthy racket. I know things about it that might bring a blush to the cheek of more than one president.'

Gary was stunned. 'You're joking.'

LaMonte shrugged, but the weight of the world, or at least the Middle European part of it, never left his shoulders. 'They need the money, my friend. And what's their finest natural resource?' Behind him, Maria looked Gary straight in the eye, lolled her legs wide open and pointed contemptuously at her crotch. 'Their women.'

Still locking eyes, she picked up her bottle and ran her long, strong tongue lasciviously around the head.

Gary wrenched his eyes away from her with a superhuman effort. He scrabbled desperately in his jacket pocket – for once in his life, what was in the pocket of a jacket seemed more important than what was on the label – and handed Ava Kavan's photograph and letter to Johnson. 'I need your help – LaMonte. It's my friend's sister – this girl. He thought she'd married an American and

312

gone to live in the US. Now it turns out there was no such person, no such zone. Return to sender. He's sure she's caught up in this skin trade. Is there anything you can do when you get back to Washington? To stop the trade at your end – or to trace her?'

'There may be.' LaMonte looked at the letter, then at the photo. 'Damn it, there *must* be.' He pushed a pen and paper towards Gary. 'Give me your friend's number. We've got to move fast. Next week I'll be back home, and I can keep an eye on DC. But then there's New York, Chicago ... and there's Mexico.' He looked bleak, beyond despair.

'Mexico?' Gary didn't catch his drift. 'What happens in Mexico?'

LaMonte gave a bitter laugh. 'Son, don't even ask me.'

'Snuff films,' pronounced Maria, by now drunk beyond belief. She made a throat-slitting motion, then hiccuped once more. 'Wham, bam, blam and goodbye Charlie.' She raised her bottle. 'Bottoms up. As they say down Mexico way.'

LaMonte winced, facing Gary, but was smiling patiently as he turned to look at her. 'You're drunk, my darling. Why don't you go and lie down?'

Maria oozed on to her feet, clutching her bottle like a buoy. Or a boy. 'Only if Mr First lies on top of me.'

Johnson's voice was still patient, like a martyred mother. 'Maria, you're *very* drunk, darling. Please go and lie down or I shall have to tie you down.'

She snorted. 'Promises, promises!' she muttered, weaving from the room.

LaMonte watched her go, still benevolent, and then turned back to Gary in garrulous mode. 'They're a capricious people, Gary – like children, in many ways. They look like us, but they're innocent. And, like children, the dirtier they talk the less they really know. Look at Maria.' Gary only wished he could, preferably drunk and naked. 'A child drunk on stolen champagne. Talk, talk, talk – all dirty, all meaningless. Fantasies. I love her dearly, but I take the kid's prattle with a fair-sized Siberian salt-mine, I can tell you.' He stood up; so did Gary. LaMonte shook his hand, very sincerely. 'Thank you for sharing this with me, Gary. You know, I thought you were a boy – but it took a man to come here.' LaMonte twinkled horribly.

'You've got a crush on her, haven't you – but let's face it, she's got a crush on you. A schoolgirl crush, nothing nasty. Am I right – or am I right?' He grinned then, and capped the grotesque performance with a wink. 'Just as well she's being shipped out.'

'It's me. I must see you. One time before we go.'

'Maria!' The sound of his own voice shocked him in its shrillness. He looked around his living room guiltily, horribly aware of how it lacked a woman's touch; the angry stink of depilatory, the ghostly footprints of talcum, the used tampon in the bin. Instead it was overbearingly masculine; the fetid socks on the breakfast table, the crazy foam of the shaving canister obscuring the mirror, the disgustingly violated tissues in the wastepaper basket. Of course men and women were both disgusting, in their own way. But the sort of yuckiness that a woman's presence brought with it was at least comforting, while male yuckiness was so damn *bleak*. 'Maria!' he whispered, thrilled. 'It's really you?'

'No, this is a recording. In ten seconds it will

self-destruct, leaving only a moist stain of desire on the sofa where I sit.' She gurgled lusciously.

'You mean it? I can really see you again?'

'Just this once. It can't hurt now. My bags are packed, and my ticket to ride is under my virginal pillow.'

His heart hurt. But his dick was already making plans and heading for the hills. 'I bet you kiss it every night.'

'You're joking. I roll it up and jerk off on it, don't I?' There appeared to be some sort of mucous in her voice. Gary shivered. She became suddenly became businesslike. 'Same time, same place, same room.'

'Same sex?'

'You never know. I might have a surprise for you. Or two.'

The line went dead.

Gary went to the bathroom, and toyed with the affections of a whole roll of toilet paper.

Katya unlocked the door of the room at the Hotel Evropa, smiled silently and padded away. It struck him that she had always served silently and smilingly as the keeper of their flame of fucking, and he wished he had had the chance to talk to her properly at some point. About the important things in life; like what had Maria been like at twelve, what was her favourite colour, had all the boys at their school been in love with Maria? Well, he would never know.

He pushed the door opened, walked in and closed it quickly and quietly, as protocol had always demanded. And turning around, lit by the glow of sixteen candles, he saw something which had once been his fantasy. And old sex fantasies, like the past, are a foreign country.

A beautiful Czech girl, the perfect stranger of spoilt Western wank fodder, her hair tucked under a black bowler hat, her milky, silky body bound briefly by black lace bra and pants, suspenders and stockings, her feet in black high heels, was on all fours, kneeling over a mirror the size of a table top, smiling up at him.

My God – what would Marco say? It was all he could register. The beautiful wet dream in duplicate on the floor had nothing to do with Maria Vachss, beloved of Gary First, affianced of LaMonte Johnson, a sad and sensitive young woman whose instinct for survival had convinced her (and a cast of thousands) that she was a cold and calculating bitch. This, the thing on the floor, was nothing but a mirage.

Oh yeah? – his cock begged to differ, and sprang up, ready to make good its escape from the po-faced prig it had found itself wearing – sod you, mate, I'll see you later. *Masturbator*!

Get *down*! Gary almost audibly hissed – and his erection magically evaporated as love and its pure benediction fell on him once more. He went forward, his right hand out, to help her up. 'Oh, Maria,' he said sadly. 'What a beautiful thing to do.'

'You don't like it.' Her voice was empty of everything, especially questions like that.

'It's like a view on a postcard – like some beautiful memory from the past. But it has nothing to do with us. With now.'

Maria regarded him coolly, not moving from her canine crouch; then she looked at his hand. It occurred to him that she might bite it; then he dismissed this as a probability, given her loathing of cheap metaphors. Instead she considered, filled her mouth and spat a huge pool of saliva on to his palm. She looked up at him with sparkling, mocking eyes.

'Take down my pants, rub that spit on my asshole and stick your dick all the way up it. And then say that.'

Some things were just not worth fighting, he mused, as his cock sprang up to salute such tenacious female initiative. He kneeled behind her, pulled her pants around her ankles, slammed his saliva'd palm against her anus and tried his luck. She tensed, then yielded, and he slid half the way in.

She groaned and said something in Czech under her breath.

He looked over her cold shoulder, down into the mirror, and saw her beautiful narrow face contorted – in either pain or pleasure; he wasn't dumb enough to think the two came for the price of one any more.

'Is it good for you?' he whispered tenderly, appalled at his choice of words, and his lack of choice over his finer feelings.

She groaned in a unique synthesis of ecstasy and irritation. 'Don't talk, First, just fuck. That's what you're good at.'

Her wish was his command; his dominance, her

dalliance. Back and forth he moved in her ass, like a miner working a seam, bent on breaking through to that black gold of her precious mind. He worked, sweating, until she stiffened and hissed, as though someone had tried to do her out of money at the market.

'Keep still, keep *still*!' she barked – then tensed, yowled and relaxed. She fell at ease for a few moments, then threw a smile over her shoulder; he caught it, like a bride's black bouquet. Yes, little boy, you can be the next to have a broken heart.

'Can I come now?' he muttered in her ear.

'Come up my ass? But that's how journalists are born!'

The raw power of the first sentence cancelled out the sarcasm of the second, and he came in a tourniquet of tension and taboo before collapsing on her and with her, like runaway horse and rider refusing the final jump – losers and *still* champs.

They lay recovering their breath for a few minutes.

'Do you want a cigarette?' she asked finally.

'No. I've given up.'

'Gary, you'll never give up.'

She laughed, almost nostalgically; it chilled him

to realise that she was already thinking of him in the past tense, that she would sit on her Washington terrace on lazy Sundays, nursing a spritzer and smoking a Marlboro, and think of him not just without pain but even with a bittersweet sort of pleasure – The Boy I Left Behind, for My Brilliant Career as a Trophy Wife. He cursed himself for falling in love with a woman who thought in women's magazine straplines. And he felt suddenly angry that he was still in his twenties and already a fading sepia snapshot in some bitch's back pages.

Spreading her buttocks with one hand, he held her hands above her head with the other and re-entered her savagely. She screamed, but his hand was already on her mouth.

He was pumping her like a power drill when he felt foreign fingers reach back between his legs and grasp his testicles. She squeezed, with the gloves off. And as he passed out in a white heat of agony, Gary reflected that this was surely a fitting end to their singular physical friendship.

17

He skated on a smirk into the canteen and slid his tray along the rails as though it was sasparilla, straight. Catching up with it at the serving hatch, he opened his mouth to say something ballsy and male-bondy about there being no stopping them now they had American might on their side. But the words popped on his lips, foolish as bubble gum. Where Tomas should have been, a surly carrot-topped geek stared sullenly back at him, ladle raised truculently as Gary thrust his tray forward and shook his head at the same time.

The man rolled his eyes. Obviously, like Maria, a graduate of the Václav Havel Charm School. 'Come on! You want, you don't want!'

'Don't want,' Gary gaped. Abandoning the tray like a murder weapon, he turned around and stared wildly through the tables, looking for someone. There he was; the smooth dark head bent solemnly over the back copy of *Viz*.

'Alexander!' Gary grabbed his shoulder and slid into the spare seat. 'Where's Tomas?'

Alexander shrugged. 'The Golem with the goulash? I don't know. Sick, maybe? Had to have his bandages removed?'

'Will you help me, mate? I need to call him.'

'So call him.' Alexander held on to his *Viz* stubbornly. 'Get his number from the kitchen. What's up? You want to sue him for dropping that coffee on you? This isn't America, you know.'

'It's not that.' Gary lowered his voice. 'Please. Help me and I'll tell you later. I can't be seen calling him.' He looked at the magazine. 'Listen – when I go back to Blighty for my first break, I'll get you every issue of that ever printed. I promise.'

He looked at the young man, sure of success.

Alexander sighed – art had won out over convenience once more. His lunch unfinished – though Gary had noticed of Czech cuisine that it wasn't always easy to know what you should eat and what you should leave, so maybe this was not so – he got to his feet. 'OK, gringo. Hang about.'

Gary watched him go to the hatch, signal to a friendly server – not Laughing Boy – and speak to him. The server thought and spoke; Alexander whipped out his writing gear. Then he nodded at the man, pocketed the paper and walked from the canteen. A moment later, Gary followed him.

They walked silently down the corridor, not speaking, into Alexander's office. Alexander held out the number, looking serious, as Gary closed the door.

Gary shook his head, backing away from the piece of paper. 'Please. No. You call.'

Alexander looked at him steadily. He picked up the phone, looked at the paper and dialled. Gary heard the phone being picked up far away, and a woman's loud, emotional voice recite the number.

Alexander never stopped staring at him as he spoke.

'Good day. May I speak to Tomas Kavan, please?'

Far away, there were tears, and a torrent of a foreign tongue.

'I see. I am so very sorry. Please forgive me for bothering you in your grief. He was a good man.'

Alexander put down the receiver slowly, and his eyes were the eyes of a child looking at broken promises as he said, 'Oh, gringo. What have you *done?*'

LaMonte turned to him, smiling silkily. 'Good evening, Gary. I was expecting you earlier.'

'I'm on Czech time now.' Gary stumbled like a drunk into the centre of the beautiful room, staring at him. 'Late for everything and slow on the uptake.' He pointed at LaMonte with a shaky finger. 'Government white slave trade be buggered. It's just *you*. This whole thing. The lying, and the kidnapping, and the killing – a rich man's board game, played with real people. A bored man's board game.' The finger raised and steadied itself, pointing straight between Johnson's eyes. 'And you murdered my friend.'

LaMonte shrugged. 'Not me *personally*. This is the Naked City, Mr First – there are a million guns for hire within its walls. Whores and hoodlums walk the beautiful cobbled streets of this orchidaceous place; human garbage, just like back home in my own fair town – the nation's capital of Washington DC. They're the same everywhere. The less of them the better. If you insist on a crude explanation. Myself, I find life and death a far more ... *complex* business.'

Gary lunged at him then. But Johnson stopped him with a tiny revolver, looking straight at him with its deadly single eye.

'But I *will* kill you personally, if I have to. Go home now, son, and sleep on this. You're an ambitious young man, we both know that. You need friends. And you can't prove a thing.'

'I'll get you for this.' He was sickeningly aware of how pathetic the words sounded – in this context, in this compound – the words of primary playground pique. But he could hardly threaten a representative of the US Government with the merciless might of the BBC World Service, could he?

'Ever heard of diplomatic immunity, Mr First?'

LaMonte Johnson was smiling dreamily now, everything sewn up – including the mouth of his enemy, it would seem. He gestured vaguely with the gun, ethereal as a poet who had just written his masterpiece. 'You, young man, irritate me, I have decided. Go now. Or your people will have to send you back to dear old Blighty in a Pak-A-Pet.'

As finished as he would ever be, Gary turned to go. Then it hit him, and he wheeled round, his defeat defeated.

'Where's Maria?'

LaMonte yawned; Gary could almost tell the blood group of the stuff on his teeth. 'Taking a nap. She has to be fresh for her trip, you understand.'

'What trip?'

'We're going home tomorrow. At least, *I'm* going home.' He smiled and blew a kiss down the gun's barrel as though blowing a kiss to a beloved. '*She's* going for a little vacation, in Mexico. Lovely at this time of year, I hear.' He took a soft yellow cloth from his desk drawer and began to polish the gun with it. Silently, but speaking volumes, he fitted a silencer. 'Yes, she'll knock 'em dead down there. Blonde hair. Big tits.' He flashed a supremely gleeful grin at Gary, happy as a sandboy. 'Even after she's dead they'll be queueing up to – '

The blood beat a crazed tattoo through Gary's head, and he looked wildly around the room for some obscure weapon. Then, the end of his tether seeming to hit him with the half-brick tied to it, he slumped once more, turned on his heel and skulked towards the door.

But as he passed it, he hit the light switch. The blazing chandelier disappeared into the darkness that would soon ripen to dusk. Before it did, Gary leaped on the man who was spluttering 'What the – ' and showed him.

There was a muffled shot, and the light went on. Gary stood; one hand on the switch, and the other on salvation. The discreet little grey number had crossed the floor, and now nestled ingenuously in his hand. 'Who – me? Help that SOB on the floor there?' the perfect surprised O of its mouth seemed to say.

LaMonte, on all fours, was scuffling under the desk.

'Over here, big boy,' said Gary grimly, and very softly.

LaMonte peered over the desk at him, stunned.

Gary was breathing heavily, almost ecstatically. His eyes gleamed. 'Get up, you pig. Get on your feet – two feet. Try to walk like a man, at least. You fucking *animal*.'

Johnson stood up slowly, holding Gary's stare. 'You're making a big mistake, Gary.' Call the nutter by his name. Establish human contact. What a fucking sick joke. 'You're threatening a citizen of the United States of America.' There appeared to be a lump in the loony's throat, and Gary wondered for a moment if he was going to whip out a flag and kiss it. America, the sentimental sadist. It all added up. But instead he pulled himself together. 'On United States territory,' he added hastily, showing what to Gary appeared to be an exaggerated respect for property and the laws of trespass, considering his nuts were on a knife edge.

'I'll do more than threaten him!' Gary heard himself cackle in a strange Cockney accent – he knew not from whence it came – like some souped-up and psychotic stand-up comic.

'If I call the guards, you're dead, Gary.' Johnson's voice was shaky. 'They'll shoot you on sight. And be within their rights. *They* won't take time out to dialogue with you.'

'Shoot me on sight?' Gary mocked in a sing-song Yankee whine. 'Not if I've got this here *piece* up your all-American *butt* they won't!' Suddenly he was deadly serious. 'Where's Maria?'

Johnson couldn't resist it. Contempt conquered even his survival instinct. 'Just follow your nose.'

Gary hoped for the best, aimed for Johnson's right hand and squeezed the trigger. Bull's eye. Johnson looked down at his shattered hand, the blood draining from his face into the bargain. He looked at Gary with mute reproach, as if begging to be told what he had done to earn such punishment.

'Don't yell,' said Gary quietly. 'And don't whine. You just insulted the woman I love. Go on – do it again. So I get the set.'

'You're crazy.' The American was terrified.

'No – I'm English.' Gary spoke reasonably and almost gently, as though trying hard to keep his temper and make a fool see sense. 'Us and the Czechs, we go back a long way. We owe them one.' He laughed softly. 'You wouldn't understand – it's a European thing.' He walked round the desk, grabbed Johnson around the neck and held the gun to his head. 'Take me to your fiancé. *Now*.'

'This way,' choked LaMonte, taking a ring of keys from his Ivy League pocket – poison Ivy! – and attempting vainly to jerk his hand-held head towards a pair of ornate doors which Gary had presumed led into a large closet. Together they struggled towards them, unwilling partners in an infernal three-legged race.

Gary released him for long enough to unlock the doors, then grabbed him once more before flinging them open and swearing to God.

Maria was naked and not quite dead, unconscious but breathing – too – deeply, spreadeagled on a small bed. Her wrists and ankles were tied down and large whip welts made brief bikinis of grotesque modesty across her breasts and groin. There was an empty champagne bottle shoved up her.

'Only the best until the end for my little peasant princess,' Johnson couldn't stop himself from sniggering. Did he have a death wish, or what?

Almost casually, Gary raised the gun and smashed it down on the American's head before shoving him into the corner furthest from the doors. He kept the gun trained on him to the best of his abilities while he untied Maria. 'Stay there, you scumbag. I'll deal with you later.'

The bonds were done; he began to shake her by the shoulders, first with one hand and then with two. 'Maria! Maria, wake up, you dozy cow! Don't leave me!' What a dumb thing to say!

Johnson staggered to his feet and made a run for it; Gary shot him in the left foot, though more by chance than by design. He collapsed obediently back into his corner, whimpering.

Gary stood up and looked calculatingly at Maria. She was out for the count – only one thing for it. He bent down and hoisted her bodily over his shoulder; the bottle fell with an obscene plop on to the bed.

Gary scowled at Johnson. 'You're lucky I don't give you this up the ass, mate. Come on. Up. Walkies. You're playing gooseberry.' He jerked the gun at LaMonte, who was rising painfully on to his feet. 'A long walk. All the way back to Blighty, if need be.'

'I've got guards,' LaMonte warned him, shuffling towards them.

'So? I've got *you*, babe.' Gary balanced Maria on one shoulder, and held the gun in the right hand that steadied her legs. With the other he grabbed Johnson around the neck, forcing him to bend his knees and stagger, the gun to his head. 'Move it!'

Two armed and uniformed guards were chewing gum and looking at a Claudia Schiffer calendar – simultaneously! – when the odd threesome stumbled out into the corridor. They dropped their girl and went for their weapons. But Johnson's voice stopped them in their tracks.

'Don't shoot! It's loaded! He's crazy!'

'Or "*He's* loaded, *it's* crazy",' remarked Gary pleasantly, partly to himself, partly to Johnson and partly to the guards. It occurred to him that he was behaving strangely, almost frivolously. But he comforted himself with the probability that crazy behaviour in a crazy situation might be a good way of staying sane. God, he was thinking like one of Maria's you-can-do-it-sucker books! That was it; he'd have to marry her, to change her reading habits. A good solid course of Kundera might be favourite, combining national pride with a nice range of legover side benefits.

He grinned grotesquely at the guards. 'Hear that? That's me. Crazy English! See this woman? She's Czech! Out for the count! Drugged up to the eyeballs by big white bwana here. He was going to sell her to the spics for dog food! He'll sell your sisters, too, if you let him! Your mothers, if he gets desperate, and your daughters, when you have them! So don't shoot me! *English*! Winston Churchill! Bobby Moore! Beatles! Princess Diana! MARGARET THATCHER!'

With the end of his mantra, he fell through the street doors, still dragging LaMonte and carrying Maria. They were both completely docile. A fat lot of good that did him. He realised that Johnson was silent now because he knew that Gary had nowhere to go from here. The game, such as it was, was up.

'Oh God, what now?' At the other end of the street, a police car purred into action. He *felt* Johnson smile. No proof, no blame. A lover's quarrel or some sex game would explain the marks on Maria. And Gary would be left holding the gun. 'Please God. Beam me up, Scottie.'

He was staring at the slowly approaching police car, transfixed. He didn't hear the sleek, dark blue

Daimler slink up behind him. But he heard the voice, the voice which made him think instantly of Russian roulette and untipped cigarettes and losing your job to some little jerk whose ass you were fated to save, if not to fuck, one fine day.

'Hello, ducky. Want to come for a ride with a nice man?'

In the driving seat of the Daimler, a beautiful blonde Slav boy in a grey uniform stared straight ahead. In the passenger seat, leaning out of the window and smoking a Rothman's with smiling insouciance, was Edmond Crichton.

Gary felt his knees buckle, and tears come to his eyes. LaMonte sensed it, and began to struggle as the police car approached.

Gary looked to his left, to his right, and decided which way to jump. 'Edmond!' He screamed it, his voice full of childish glee and elation, like the way Jenny Agutter yelled 'Daddy! My daddy!' at the end of *The Railway Children*. He'd always loved that film. Shoving the struggling LaMonte to the ground, he hurled Maria in through the open back door and dived in on top of her. The young Slav had the car going at full speed before Edmond even got the door closed behind them.

The guards were firing now, but half-heartedly, looking down at the agonised LaMonte with something between fear and loathing. The police were chasing, but not gaining. And the British Embassy loomed ahead.

Chattering like a monkey, Gary was squeezing and hugging the silent Maria like a maniac.

Edmond leaned over the back of his seat and smiled indulgently. 'So. You've been keeping your head down, I take it?'

18

Maria was dead.

Sure she was breathing — but he knew she was dead. Or in a coma, at the very least.

They had been at the Embassy for more than half an hour and he had tried everything in the book, respiration-wise. Nothing would wake her. Nothing ever would.

Edmond put his head around the door of the small, functional bedroom. 'Any luck, love bucket?'

'No. She's dead.' Gary's voice broke, and he burst into tears.

'Dear heart!' Edmond pranced around the door in an agitated manner and stood there looking at him anxiously, his own plump lower lip trembling in sympathy. Tentatively he put a hand out to touch Gary's shoulder. And the boy went wild, throwing himself into the man's arms and sticking there like glue until Edmond was forced to hug him.

'There, there,' he muttered miserably, not knowing what was etiquette in such circumstances. A young hetero beauty weeping in one's arms for a girlfriend in a coma! – they didn't cover this one in Old Queen's Dating Dos and Don'ts, that was for sure. 'There – um, *there*.'

'She's dead!' shrieked Gary suddenly.

'She is not!'

'Is so!'

'Gary!' Edmond held him at arm's length and spoke sharply. 'You've got to pull yourself together! We're not out of trouble yet, you know. What exactly have you tried with her?'

'Everything,' said Gary sulkily. 'Cold water. Got a bit of black coffee down her. Heart massage

– and I didn't think *once* about what great tits she's got. That's how much I love her.' He snivelled, and wiped his nose on his sleeve. 'I even slapped her – it hurt me more than it hurt her, I can tell you.'

Edmond shook his head solemnly. 'Like youth itself, flagellation is wasted on the young. That's always been my only objection to corporal punishment in the public school system, I believe.' He twinkled coyly at Gary. 'Haven't you forgotten the obvious?'

'Come again?'

Edmond sighed. 'Why don't you *kiss* her, dear boy?'

Gary looked down at the motionless girl. It was a long shot, but well worth trying. He went to the bed and bent over it, tasting her lipsticky fragrant lips and metallic breath – the taste of love, as he would always think of this mixture of bacteria and perfume.

And then her long grey jazz eyes opened.

'Where am I?' she whispered.

'England,' Gary gasped. 'The British Embassy, I mean.'

'Welcome back to the land of the living, Miss

Maria!' Edmond swooped down and sat beside her, at which the bed protested loudly. 'And didn't you miss all the fun! Your young man, you will be interested to hear, is due to wake up tomorrow, or next week, or whenever they let the cat out of the diplomatic bag, as a fully fledged hero. Having shot and injured a representative of the US Government in his own Embassy, no less, and snatched you from the jaws of death. Tomorrow he's to be taken by Her Maj's Ambassador to Prague and put on a sealed train to the English Channel, and from there on a hovercraft back to Blighty. Pure George MacDonald Fraser.' He batted his eyelashes at the startled Maria. 'All it needs to complete the picture is an imperious, wanton, flaxen-haired Mittel Euro femme fatale to share the sleeping car.'

'I'm not a femme fatale.' Maria buried her face in her hands. 'I'm a walking, talking, pouting, shouting disaster area.' She looked up at Gary, appalled. 'You'll lose your job?'

He nodded.

Edmond clasped his hands operatically and smiled from ear to ear. 'Ah, but look what he found!'

19

Gary First stretched out to his full length along the bottom bunk of the sleeping car speeding towards England, and rustled *The European* languidly.

Like a peculiarly beautiful Best of Breed responding to the call of Pavlov, Maria Vachss' face appeared upside down over the edge of the upper bunk. In that moment his vision blurred, and he saw her as she would one day be; at thirty, a little bitter and puffy from too many cocktails and too few career opportunities; at forty, with a new, ancient, streamlined beauty, carrying the weight of European history in the bags under her eyes; at fifty, still the most beautiful girl in the world. Then his vision cleared, and she was once more a girl at her optimum max perf of pulchritude. But he knew he had seen into the future and never once loved her less, and he was happy.

He grinned at her. The yard of blonde hair falling straight down behind the beautiful upside-down head with the solemn expression was, amongst other things, funny.

'Gary,' she said solemnly.

'Maria,' he said, parodying her.

'Twenty years from now, will you accuse me of ruining your life?'

He stood up and threw his newspaper through the open window, knowing he would never buy the boring bastard again. He *was* a European now, for better or worse, and had no need of phoney poses. 'Definitely. At least once during the next eighty years. Probably when I'm drunk and maudlin. But every other day, in every other way, I'll prove to you until I'm blue in the face that my pathetic life only started when I met you.'

She sat up and swung her legs over the side of the bunk. 'But your career – '

'My *career*?' He went to the bunk and put his hands on her waist, looking up at her. 'My *career*, when this little darling breaks? White slave trade, American imperialist evil, beautiful blonde snatched from the jaws of death, white wedding?' He laughed with sheer delight and squeezed her tight. 'Maria, you're my meal ticket! My little cashcow!' Then a sly look came into his face. 'Will you do something for me?'

She looked him in the eye, completely blunt and lascivious. 'Anything.'

He touched her feet. 'Please. I beg you. Just throw away these disgusting shoes.'

She threw back her beautiful head and laughed like a child, no longer cruel. Then she tore off her famous white stilettos, with which she had walked all over his heart, all over his life, and cast them through the open window of the speeding train. He vaulted up into the bunk beside her as the train went into its last pitch-black tunnel.

They sped away from a Europe intent on tearing

itself apart, back to England. As they emerged into light, an express bore down upon the shoes, destroying them forever, along with their legend: MADE IN CZECHOSLOVAKIA.